THE M'DOK SHIP,
SHIELDS RAISED,
MOVED FORWARD . . .

"It appears we struck them after all," the sensor officer said. "My readings indicate loss of warp speed capability, power output in their engineering section down by fifty percent."

Ahead of them, the main screen showed the *Centurion*, a silver dot moving slowly, erratically, around the planet below.

"Close on them," the captain said harshly. He turned his back on the weapons officer and took his seat on the command cushion. "Once we are within range, you have my leave to destroy them."

"Then Tenara will be ours for the taking."

Look for STAR TREK Fiction from Pocket Books

Star Trek: The Original Series

Star Trek: The Next Generation

POCKET BOOKS

New York   London   Toronto   Sydney   Tokyo

#8

STAR TREK®
THE NEXT GENERATION

THE CAPTAINS' HONOR

DAVID AND DANIEL DVORKIN

POCKET BOOKS

New York   London   Toronto   Sydney   Tokyo

An *Original* Publication of POCKET BOOKS

POCKET BOOKS, a division of Simon & Schuster Inc.
1230 Avenue of the Americas, New York, NY 10020

ISBN: 0-671-68487-6

First Pocket Books printing September 1989

10 9 8 7 6 5 4 3 2 1

POCKET and colophon are trademarks of
Simon & Schuster Inc.

Printed in the U.S.A.

To my coauthor

Historian's note: This adventure takes place shortly after the death of Lieutenant Tasha Yar, in the first-season STAR TREK: The Next Generation episode *Skin of Evil*. Readers may also wish to consult the original series episode *Bread and Circuses* for further information on Magna Roman society.

Prologue

SILENCE.

That is the one overriding characteristic of space—not the immensity, or the beauty of the star-flecked blackness, but the silence.

The M'dok battleship *Restoration* drifted soundlessly into orbit around Tenara, a shining speck in the ebony void.

On the command deck, however, there was the sound of playful chatter.

"Our greatest victory," commented the helmsman.

The captain nodded. "If this raid succeeds," he promised, sinking back onto his command cushion, "the heads of our victims will adorn your cabins for twelve twelvedays."

"Great honor," the weapons officer purred. "Just three twelvedays ago, my year-wife bore a new litter. The little ones will enjoy the delicacies we bring them, I think."

Even now, the captain knew, back home all the M'dok little ones were yowling with hunger. Time was growing ever shorter for all his people.

A stranger looking at the M'dok captain would see

none of this tension. They would note only his ramrod-straight posture, the polished sheen of his uniform and blaster, and, if they were conversant with M'dok culture, the orange and green horizontal banding around his neck that marked him as one of the higher caste. If they were not conversant with M'dok culture, they might easily mistake the captain for a member of any of the other feline races common to so many class-M planets. Which would be a mistake— for unlike the other, more typically gentle feline races, the M'dok had once ruled this entire quadrant of space. Ruled with an iron fist—that is, until the coming of the Federation had robbed them of their colonies, and confined them to their own stellar system. Now, with this ship, the captain intended to put right that ancient wrong.

"Alarm," said the sensor officer suddenly, his back arched. "A starship is approaching, falling into orbit from one-eleven."

"They request we identify ourselves," added the communications officer.

"Radio silence!" the captain snapped. "Categorize."

"Federation—constitution-class starship," replied the sensor officer. "Considerably smaller than our vessel, sir."

As we expected. The captain nodded with a smile of satisfaction.

The *Restoration* was larger, more powerful than all but the great Galaxy-class starships of the Federation, and there were only a handful of those. *Too few to waste on such a backwater planet, certainly.*

He studied the readouts in front of him, scratching the edge of the console absentmindedly. Power-consumption levels indicated that the *Restoration* outgunned the starship by a factor of at least four to one.

Disappointing. It won't even be a fight.

His officers crouched over their stations expectantly, awaiting their captain's orders.

"Sir!"

It was the communications officer who had spoken—a disturbing breach of protocol, considering his youth and inexperience.

The captain turned, ready to admonish the young officer.

The communications post was at the rear of the great open command area. The youth was standing there, back to his captain, his tail straightened, his posture indicating great agitation. "The starship has identified itself as the *Centurion!*"

At once the captain felt the fur on the back of his neck rise. All thoughts of censuring the youth were gone, replaced by an excitement he knew the rest of his crew shared.

The Centurion. To destroy this ship . . .

There could be no better way to prove to the Highest of M'dok the worth of the *Restoration*—and its captain.

He sprang off his command cushion and stalked the length of the deck to the weapons officer's side.

"Unsheathe our weapons, but wait for my order to strike."

"Aye."

"Another request for identification, sir," the communications officer reported.

"Do we have visual?" the captain asked.

"Yes, Captain."

"Then put it on-screen!" the captain snapped.

The view of space at the front of the M'dok command area disappeared—to be replaced by the image of a human, sharp-featured, of middle age, in what the captain assumed was Starfleet uniform.

". . . repeating our request that you identify yourselves. This is Captain Lucius Aelius Sejanus of the *Centurion.*"

The M'dok captain leaned forward.

Sejanus himself, and the *Centurion.* Even within the M'dok Empire, cut off by the accursed Federation from galactic civilization these past two hundred years, the victories of this captain, of this ship, were well-known. The defeat of the J'Nakan convoy, destruction of the Romulan war fleet in the Adharan system . . .

Yes, the *Centurion* would be a worthy opponent and a most worthy test for the *Restoration.*

"Very well, Captain Sejanus," the captain said softly. "We will identify ourselves." He clamped a hand on the weapons officer's shoulder. "Full phasers . . . now!"

The weapons officer pulled the phaser lever. Triple bolts of red-yellow light seared the darkness . . .

. . . and disappeared harmlessly into the Tenaran atmosphere.

"What happened?" the captain hissed angrily.

The weapons officer looked as angry at himself. "They dodged, sir, and disappeared."

"So quickly? Where?"

The sensor officer scratched his cushion in frustration.

"Sensor traces indicate that they entered the atmosphere, sir, but I can no longer track them."

"The atmosphere . . ." the captain said thoughtfully. "Perhaps we struck them after all?"

"Possible," said the sensor officer, "but unlikely."

Then he yowled, "Directly below us, sir!"

"Helm—hard left! Fire phasers again!"

The *Restoration* shuddered as the engines and artificial-gravity units whined—but it escaped the photon torpedo fired by the Federation ship.

"They just sent a tight-beam subspace transmission," the communications officer reported. "A call for assistance."

"It will do them no good," replied the captain. "Helmsman, take us out of orbit—put some hunting distance between us."

The *Restoration* leapt ahead, leaving the Federation ship still mired in Tenara's atmosphere and gravity well.

"Sejanus has earned his reputation," the captain acknowledged. "But a reputation will do no good against this ship."

"Picking them up ahead of us," the sensor officer said.

Now the main viewscreen was filled with the image of space—and ahead of them, the *Centurion,* a silver dot, moving slowly, erratically around the planet below.

"It appears we struck them after all," the sensor officer said. "My readings indicate loss of warp-speed capability, power output in their engineering section down by fifty percent."

"Close on them," the captain said harshly. He savored the moment, committing it to memory, so that for years to come he could tell of his defeat of the Federation's greatest warrior.

The captain turned his back on the weapons officer and took up his seat on the command cushion. "Once we are within range, you have my leave to destroy them."

"Then Tenara will be ours for the taking."

Chapter One

ACCORDING TO THE REGULATIONS MANUAL he had so recently finished reviewing, a starship bridge officer receiving an emergency call for assistance should pass the message on to the senior officer on the bridge in a calm, detached manner.

But when Lieutenant Worf received the distress signal from the *Centurion,* he responded not in the manner of the trained Starfleet professional, but as a Klingon warrior with a thousand generations of warrior blood running through his veins.

In other words, he yelled.

"Commander Riker!"

The *Enterprise's* first officer, who had been sitting conversing amiably with ship's counselor Deanna Troi, started forward in his chair.

Worf immediately realized he had spoken rather louder than he'd intended, and made a distinctive effort to calm down.

By the book, Lieutenant, he told himself. *By the book.*

"Sir, I am receiving a request for assistance from

the USS *Centurion*. She is in orbit around Tenara and is coming under heavy attack from an unknown assailant."

Riker jumped to his feet. "Data, how soon can we get there?"

At the ops console, the android lieutenant spoke calmly and precisely. "Two hours minimum, sir, at top warp speed. At our present rate, two days."

"Damn," Riker muttered. "Maximum warp, then. Immediately."

"Warp nine-point-six—aye, sir."

Worf knew the commander's thoughts paralleled his own. *Even at maximum warp, we'll be there in time to do nothing better than pick up the pieces. If there are any.* Worf felt the subtle sensation throughout his body as the ship accelerated.

Riker turned to Worf again. "Send a message to the *Centurion* that we're on the way."

Worf complied as Riker touched the fleet insignia on his chest and spoke again. "Captain Picard, to the bridge."

"The *Centurion*," Worf said after he had completed the transmission. "Captain Sejanus' ship."

Riker nodded. "Let's hope we get there in time."

All ships, all lives, were equally valuable, but it was difficult to believe that a ship and a commander so famous for daring exploits, so apparently invulnerable, could be destroyed. *That can't happen to legends,* Worf thought—but of course he knew better.

There were numerous examples of just such occurrences quoted in the Starfleet regulations manual.

* * *

When the call came, Jean-Luc Picard was sleeping in his cabin. Riker's voice requesting his presence on the bridge brought him awake instantly. As Picard's eyes opened, he was sliding off the bed. He pulled on his boots quickly, but without wasteful haste.

Other than his boots, he was fully dressed: he had learned years ago that it was wisest to nap fully clothed and lying atop the covers rather than under them. At first he had found his naps less than restful, but he'd adjusted and realized the truth in the old saying that a starship captain is always on duty.

Minutes later, the turbolift doors whooshed open and Picard stepped out onto the bridge. Riker turned quickly at the sound.

"Captain."

"What is it, Number One?" Picard's eyes swept over the bridge, noting the quiet efficiency of his crew.

"We just received a distress signal, sir." Riker turned. "Lieutenant Worf, play that message again."

The scene of onrushing stars on the forward viewer vanished, replaced by a hugely magnified view of a man. Behind him, Picard could see busy movement, figures passing from one side to the other, and crew positions much like those on the bridge of the *Enterprise*. The man himself was stiff, erect, proud, his gray hair cropped close to his head.

"This is Captain Lucius Aelius Sejanus of the USS *Centurion*," he said, his voice beautifully modulated and resonant, each word carefully formed. "We are in orbit about the planet Tenara and have just come under attack by a powerfully armed unknown assailant. I request immediate assistance from any Federation or allied vessel within range of Tenara. If you are unable to come to our aid, I request that you pass this message along to the nearest Federation starbase or outpost." The image faded, replaced by the starfield.

"Lucius Sejanus," Picard said softly. He stared at the screen for a long moment, as if fascinated by the afterimage in his mind. Finally he tore his eyes away. "Status, Number One?"

"We received that message about fifteen minutes ago, sir. We increased to top warp speed immediately, but even so we won't reach Tenara for almost two more hours. I'm afraid we might get there too late to help."

Picard nodded. "Still, Number One, your swift action maximizes the chance that we'll be able to do some good. Does Captain Sejanus know we're coming?"

"We sent out a response immediately, sir, but there's been no reply."

The implications of that hung in the air. After a moment, Picard managed a half-smile. "If anyone in Starfleet has a chance of surviving such an attack, Number One, it's Captain Sejanus and the *Centurion*." He wheeled about, heading for the captain's ready room off the main bridge. "I'll want to see all staff officers in the meeting room in half an hour. And let me know the instant you hear anything from the *Centurion*."

"Tenara," Jean-Luc Picard said, "lies on the frontier between the Federation and the M'dok Empire. The Tenarans requested membership in the Federation seven years ago, but it's only within the last year that they were able to join us. The delay was caused by M'dok objections to what they saw as the Federation's expansion into their sphere of influence. The situation was resolved only by years of delicate negotiations." Picard stood, and began pacing back and forth in front of the spectacular view of the onrushing starfield that dominated the meeting room. His senior officers —Riker, Data, Worf, Chief Engineer Geordi La Forge, and ship's counselor Deanna Troi—were seated around the conference table in front of him.

"One very important item of the treaty between us regarding Tenara," the captain went on, "is that, while Tenara is a full member of the Federation, we will continue to regard the surrounding space as unclaimed territory. Recently, however, the Tenarans have come under attack—by hostile ships we believe to be M'dok."

"So nothing has changed, has it, Captain?" Geordi said bitterly. "They're still up to their old tricks. We negotiate with them, but it does no good. A peace treaty doesn't mean anything to them."

"The present situation is still quite different from open warfare," Picard cautioned. "And you must remember that the treaty their empire signed with the Federation almost two hundred years ago was imposed on them by us. It has never sat well with them. By that treaty, we allow them only police ships, to keep peace within the small space they still control."

He looked at the assembled officers one by one. "I know that the feeling is widespread and growing in the

Federation that violence is the proper response to this violence. That's a normal reaction, I suppose. Certainly it's an emotionally satisfying one. I hope that everyone in this room is capable of stepping back from that initial reaction, though, and thinking of the consequences. That's exactly the sort of difficult task the Federation Council has had to undertake. The *Centurion* has been assigned to help the Tenarans protect their world. We will assist them in that effort when we reach Tenara—and that is all."

"Seen from a certain perspective, the M'dok attacks do make sense, sir," Data said. "Their attacks on Tenaran industry should discourage the inhabitants there from venturing out into space and carving even larger chunks out of M'dok territory."

"Fear of losing more of what little they have left— to the Tenarans or to the Federation," Counselor Troi added. "Perhaps this is their way of posting a 'Keep Out' sign."

"Why are the attacks coming now, though?" Geordi asked. "Just as Tenara has joined the Federation. Why not before, when we wouldn't have been obligated to protect Tenara?"

Picard nodded. "A question I've asked myself, Lieutenant. Unfortunately, our knowledge of the M'dok's motives is very limited. Mr. Data?"

"I have been researching, sir, but the task is most difficult. The M'dok have not permitted Federation envoys to their worlds in almost fifty years."

"Understood. Keep on it."

The intercom sounded.

"Bridge to Captain Picard. We're now within sensor range of Tenara."

"Thank you, Mr. Crusher. We're on our way."

Led by their captain, the *Enterprise* officers returned to the bridge.

On the viewscreen, Tenara was a blue-green-and-white sphere sliding away beneath the *Enterprise,* city lights glittering on the nightside and winking out as daylight raced across the planetary surface.

Captain Picard took his command chair.

"Any sign of the *Centurion,* Mr. Crusher?"

"No, sir." The young ensign studied the instrument panel in front of him. "But I am picking up traces of debris in a low orbit around Tenara."

"Thermal radiation indicates that it came from the explosion of a starship by photon torpedo approximately two hours ago," Data added, pointing at the screen, where a brilliant light had flared and then disappeared in Tenara's upper atmosphere. "That was one of the fragments."

"Then the *Centurion* . . . is gone?" Commander William Riker's question was more an assertion than a request for information.

Data responded anyway, "That is a distinct possibility, sir. I must point out, however, that the quantity of the debris is significantly larger than would be expected from a ship the size of the *Centurion.* A ship three or four times that size would, in fact, seem to be indicated."

A cautious hope grew in Picard. "Data, announce

our arrival . . . and, Lieutenant Worf, raise the shields, if you please."

"Already done, sir," the Klingon said.

Picard glanced at him with quiet amusement.

"Starfleet regulations," Worf began, "specifically state that when entering a potential combat zone—"

"Yes, Lieutenant." Picard waved off his security chief. Worf had recently developed the annoying habit of quoting from the manual quite regularly. Picard made a note to speak to him about it later.

Data spoke quietly into the ship's communication system. "This is the USS *Enterprise,* code Open Flag. Does anyone read? I repeat, this is the USS *Enterprise,* code Open Flag, does anyone read?"

There was a long silence.

Then the speakers crackled into life. "This is Captain Sejanus of the USS *Centurion.* Come in, *Enterprise.*"

There were general sounds of relief on the *Enterprise* bridge.

Picard pressed a button on his command chair and said, "This is Captain Picard. We're relieved to find you alive and unharmed, Captain. When we received your call, and found nothing but floating debris . . ."

The starfield disappeared, to be replaced by the proud and commanding man they had seen earlier. His face carried a restrained smile. "Yes, Captain. That was the ship that attacked us. Their captain was a brave opponent, but a bit . . . overconfident. Gaius Aldus"—he gestured toward one of the bridge officers, a stocky, competent-looking man currently helping a subordinate at another console—"informs me that the ship's outlines most closely matched those of the M'dok battleships in use before the treaty—although this ship was substantially larger."

"Battleships!" exclaimed Picard.

"Indeed, Captain. As you know, whenever the Federation raises the matter with them, the M'dok insist that all they have are the police ships allowed them under the treaty. Clearly they've now built at least one battleship, a vessel of military destruction, and have used it to fire on a Federation vessel."

"Captain Sejanus." Worf spoke from his station behind Picard. "You have achieved a great victory. If it was a M'dok battleship, you have defeated a ship which outgunned you by a factor of at least three."

Sejanus' gaze shifted over Picard's shoulder to the Klingon. He smiled again. "Thank you, Lieutenant. The victory, however, is not mine. It belongs to the Federation and to my crew." He nodded in satisfaction at the crew members busily working behind him.

Picard spoke again. "I would like to meet with you, Captain, to discuss how we can aid you here—and how we can prevent another confrontation between the Federation and the M'dok."

Sejanus' face darkened momentarily. "I don't think a meeting between the two of us will solve the M'dok problem, Captain Picard. However"—the *Centurion*'s captain smiled again—"I would be honored if you and your officers would join me and my crew for dinner this evening."

"That is a most generous offer, Captain—one I gladly accept." Picard shared a smile with Riker and Troi.

"Excellent! Shall we say eighteen hundred hours, then?"

"Eighteen hundred hours, Captain," Picard agreed. "We look forward to meeting you."

"The anticipation is mutual, Captain. And please —come to us by shuttlecraft. We would like to receive you in the appropriate style."

Picard nodded and Sejanus' image flickered out, replaced by a starfield.

"A most impressive man," Riker said. "And a most impressive victory."

"Agreed, Number One," Picard said, pursing his lips thoughtfully.

"If this banquet is to be a formal occasion, sir, dress uniforms would be in order."

"Hmmm?" Picard sat forward suddenly, his train of thought broken by his first officer's query.

Riker smiled. "I was suggesting dress uniforms for this banquet, sir."

"Of course, Number One. Quite right." Picard leaned back in his chair and fell silent once again.

Deanna Troi exchanged a concerned glance with Riker and turned to her captain.

"Sir," she said quietly, "you seem troubled."

"Hmmm?" Picard turned to look at his ship's counselor. "Oh, no, Counselor, it's just . . ." He hesitated, trying to put his feelings into words. "I don't feel a victory celebration is in order at the moment."

"I don't think that's what Sejanus meant by suggesting a banquet," Riker said.

Troi shook her head. "On the contrary, Will, I think there was a definite element of that in his suggestion."

"That's natural enough, Deanna," Will Riker said, his voice rising slightly. "They've just defeated a ship which heavily outgunned them. They're undoubtedly relieved to be alive—"

"It's not relief I sense from them, Will. It's satisfaction."

"Of course they're satisfied, Deanna," Riker said. "That's the whole point."

"Counselor, Number One." The captain stood suddenly, and looked down at the two officers. "We'll be able to assess the mood of the *Centurion*'s crew, as well as find out more about what happened with the M'dok ship, at dinner."

"Yes, sir," Riker said.

"Of course, Captain." Troi nodded.

"Good," Picard said. "I'll want both of you, as well as Lieutenant Worf, Chief Engineer La Forge, and Mr. Data to accompany me."

"Sir," Worf interrupted, "I believe I should remain on board the *Enterprise.*"

Picard cocked an eyebrow. "Oh?"

"Yes, sir." The Klingon folded his hands behind his back and stood at attention, then spoke, as if reciting from memory: "'In a potential combat zone, the ranking security officer—'"

"'—is advised to remain on duty whenever possible,'" Data said, completing the sentence. "Starfleet Regulation Zed Alpha-Nine. I was going to bring it up myself, sir."

"Were you?" Picard glared at the android.

"Yes, sir." Data nodded.

Picard opened his mouth to speak, but thought

better of it and turned back to Worf. "Very well, Lieutenant. I would, however, like someone from security available to talk with *Centurion* personnel."

"Of course, sir," Worf replied.

"Good. The rest of you, meet me in shuttlebay six in one hour—in full dress uniform." He nodded to Riker. "The bridge is yours, Number One."

Captain Picard entered the shuttlebay exactly fifty-eight minutes later, in full dress uniform. Troi and Riker were already there, as were Data and Geordi La Forge, chatting amiably next to the shuttlecraft.

Geordi looked distinctly uncomfortable in his dress uniform. "I know the real reason Worf didn't want to go to this dinner," he said, fingering his collar. "He didn't want to have to get into this monkey suit."

"Speaking of Worf," Riker said, scanning the airlock, "I wonder where that security officer is."

As if in answer, a young woman strode through the airlock almost at a run and stopped suddenly, directly in front of Picard and Riker. "Ensign Jenny de Luz reporting, sir." She stood at stiff attention and fixed her gaze somewhere over Picard's shoulder.

The captain and Riker exchanged an amused look.

"At ease, Ensign," Picard said.

Jenny de Luz looked to the captain to be no more than twenty-five years old. She was tall and lean, with pale skin and bright red hair, cut short in a shaggy style. *Very much like Tasha's,* Picard realized. *Probably no coincidence.*

Picard was about to object to Worf's choice. There

were plenty of other, more seasoned security personnel the Klingon could have chosen to attend the dinner in his place—and the inclusion of so junior an officer might be taken as an insult to Sejanus. Then he remembered that Jenny was from Meramar, a Federation colony with martial values similar to those of the Magna Romans.

Not a by-the-book choice, Picard realized, *but a good one nonetheless.*

He turned to Riker. "All right, Number One. Let's get under way."

The six officers took seats in the shuttlecraft, Geordi and Data in the forward section. The chief engineer guided the shuttlecraft forward through the yawning shuttlebay door and into the brilliant starfield beyond. Just visible at one corner was an even more brilliant segment of the dayside of Tenara. And precisely in the center of the scene was a gleaming point of light, brighter than any of the stars: the *Centurion,* shining in the light of Tenara's sun.

The shuttle lifted and moved forward and out into space.

The *Centurion* grew slowly larger on the shuttlecraft's viewscreen, until it filled the entire scene. The *Centurion*'s shuttlebay doors silently scrolled open, and the *Enterprise* shuttle drifted inside. Behind it, the doors closed, their resounding bang audible as the bay filled with air. When the bay was fully pressurized, human figures marched in.

Ensign Jenny de Luz looked curiously at the scene outside the shuttle. The officers of the *Centurion* were standing at attention, lined up to provide a ceremonial pathway for the visiting officers. No wonder Sejanus had wanted them to come over by shuttlecraft: this kind of ceremony wouldn't have been possible in any other part of the ship. When visitors arrived on the *Enterprise,* she knew, Captain Picard and his senior staff waited to greet them in an informal group, not lined up at attention.

And then Jenny became even more intrigued by the fact that the *Centurion* officers were dressed in armor that looked as though it had come from ancient Rome, with short straight swords at their sides. At the end of each of the two lines, there were crewmembers wearing outfits similar to those of the officers, though these men held two-meter spears and large rectangular shields. She could tell from the set of their faces and shoulders that they were enlisted security personnel.

In the briefing she'd received from Lieutenant Worf, she'd learned that most of the officers and crew aboard the *Centurion* were from the planet Magna Roma. She'd thought this unusual, until Worf had pointed up xamples of the *Intrepid* and the *Slisha,* starships that had been manned entirely by Vulcans and Tellarites, respectively, races that preferred their own company to that of others. She had also discovered that upon re-commissioning this starship, the Federation had permitted the Magna Romans to rename this ship, once the Constitution-class cruiser the *Farragut,* in keeping with their own native traditions.

After the briefing, she'd made a quick study of the

library files on Magna Roma, and was amazed at the astounding similarity between Magna Roma's history and that of Earth. *Except on Magna Roma, the Roman Empire never fell.* There were scientific theories, she knew, that said such incredible parallels were to be expected, but to actually see evidence of this . . .

It made her wonder if she was looking at a reception detail or a troupe of historical actors.

Deanna Troi gave her an amused glance, and Jenny realized that the counselor must have sensed the emotion, if not the thought.

Though perhaps she can read my mind. I've always been so open, no emotional control at all. Like when Tasha died . . . Jenny forced the thought and the memory away, and rose from her seat.

Standing at the front of the small ship, Captain Picard gave his officers a resigned smile of puzzled amusement and nodded to Geordi.

At the captain's command, the door rose slowly, revealing the full glory of the scene before them. What looked like a time-warped Roman legion was there in full array, with two especially impressive soldiers standing next to the shuttle.

Both wore ceremonial gold armor, apparently made to fit the contours of their bodies. One stood firm and held a long staff, on top of which was a golden eagle resting on a crossbar reading SPQR. The other stepped forward, his hand on his sword hilt; all the other assembled personnel remained stock-still.

His helmet covered only the top, back, and sides of his head, revealing him to be an eagle-faced man with a powerful presence, his eyes as steely as a Romulan's as he scanned the *Enterprise* officers. *Captain Sejanus,* Jenny realized.

To the young security officer he looked remarkably like Captain Jean-Luc Picard.

"Captain Picard," Sejanus said in a resonant and powerful voice. "And your staff officers: Lieutenant La Forge, Lieutenant Commander Data, Commander Riker, and Lieutenant Commander Troi." He looked at Troi appreciatively, then turned to Jenny de Luz. "Ensign, I'm afraid I don't know you."

Jenny's lips felt frozen, her mouth dry. The man's natural power of command stunned her.

"De Luz, sir. Ensign Jenny de Luz."

Sejanus smiled broadly at her, the commander giving way to the charming aristocrat. "And you wear the uniform of Starfleet Security, Jenny."

Picard interrupted. "One of my more promising young officers, Captain."

Sejanus' glance lingered on Jenny for just a second longer, and then he turned to Picard. "And now allow me to introduce my officers." His pride in them struck Jenny as almost paternal.

As Sejanus named them, the officers stepped forward, moving past the ranks of legionnaires. One by one, they marched toward Picard, their armor jangling, and halted facing the captain of the *Enterprise*. As he stamped to a halt, each Magna Roman officer saluted Picard by slapping his right fist to his chest and then shooting his hand outward, hand open, palm down, fingers stiff.

They were all male, and they were all physically impressive specimens. Each one's face betrayed a powerful, distinct personality. The ancient Roman statuary Jenny had seen in museums on her homeworld of Meramar had that characteristic. Until now, she had thought it simply the artistic style of those times. Now she thought: *My ancestors must have had that same sort of strength and presence.* She glanced over at Picard and saw a pleased smile on his face. *He admires them too.*

Their names, however, were not so distinctive. There was a plethora of Gaiuses and Juliuses and Luciuses. *And now I understand,* Jenny thought, *why the Romans so often used the first and middle names or the first and last names when addressing each other. There's no other way to avoid confusing one Roman with another!* And then she looked again at Sejanus. *But not him. You'd never address him as "Lucius" anyway, but even if you did, there'd be no question whom you meant. Even among these strong-willed men accustomed to command, he stands out. He'd stand out anywhere.*

She noticed Picard responding with a grave nod to each salute, and a slight frown of concentration, as if intent on remembering each name and the face that went with it.

When the introductions were finished at last, Sejanus said, "And now, if you'll follow me, Captain?"

Sejanus led the way down a long corridor, with Picard at his side, the two captains conversing in low tones as they went. Behind them, the officers from the

Enterprise and the *Centurion* mingled, following their captains. Jenny walked by herself, close behind Picard, on the alert without being consciously aware of it.

The corridor decorations were quite unusual for a starship: various sculptures of carved stone along the walls. Some looked old enough to be from ancient Rome itself, while others were of various centuries, up to modern times.

Geordi La Forge, who had been walking just behind Jenny, stepped forward to her side.

"Nice statues," he commented.

She nodded. "Very. Some of the newer ones, especially, look to be—"

"Bugged," Geordi said, leaning closer.

Jenny raised her eyebrows.

"Sensors right inside of them," Geordi said, lightly touching the VISOR that covered his eyes. Jenny didn't know exactly how the instrument worked, but she did know that it enabled the chief engineer to see across the electromagnetic spectrum far beyond the range of visible light.

Jenny nodded her approval. "Very clever."

"And there's a lot of activity going on behind—"

"The bulkheads. I know. I can hear them. Efficient, organized—real Romans! I like that."

The parade of officers came to a large set of double doors, which opened to let them pass.

Jenny had to suppress a gasp as they entered. The room was as large as any aboard the *Enterprise,* surprising considering the *Centurion*'s much smaller size. It was filled with nine tables, at eight of which were seated nine Magna Romans in full military regalia.

Captain Picard was also surprised. *Nine times nine,* he thought, remembering from the dim days of his schooling in France that the ancient Romans had considered nine to be the perfect number of dinner guests. How the young Jean-Luc had detested the dictatorial Monsieur du Plessis and his Latin and history classes! But now it was all coming in handy for the adult Jean-Luc.

At the center of the room was a horseshoe-shaped table of hard dark wood inlaid with abstract designs in gold and silver and precious stones. The floor was a mosaic depicting a Roman legion of old slaughtering an army of poorly armed dark-skinned warriors. The walls of the large banqueting hall contained niches for reproductions of ancient art—Greek statues alternating with Roman portrait busts.

The open end of the center table faced wide floor-to-ceiling windows showing the starfield and the curving horizon of Tenara as the planet's surface rolled constantly away beneath them. It was more beautiful than any of the manmade art inside the room, but Picard's attention was drawn more to the heavy curtains on either side of the window. They were a deep purple, and their significance, in this neo-Magna Roman setting struck him forcefully, for Monsieur du Plessis had also impressed upon him strongly that purple was a color reserved solely for the emperors of Rome.

The two captains took seats side by side at the head of the table, Picard on the right, the place of honor.

Riker sat to his captain's right, on Riker's right was Counselor Deanna Troi, and to her right, at the end of one arm of the horseshoe, was Marcus Julius Volcinius—a dark, slender, young officer who had been introduced as a cousin of Sejanus.

Opposite Marcus Volcinius, at the end of the other arm, was Data, and then Geordi La Forge and Jenny de Luz. Finally, between Jenny and Captain Sejanus, was Gaius Aldus, whom they had seen earlier on the viewscreen on the *Enterprise* bridge.

Almost immediately, the first course was set before them—an appetizer of minuscule bits of meat sitting in a clear golden broth.

Jenny stared at the small bowls, puzzled as much by the tiny pieces of meat as by the odd smell of the broth.

Sejanus smiled. "Pickled hummingbird tongues. And the broth," he explained, "is what we call liquamen, one of our most ancient sauces, and still very popular."

"Suppose I could exchange it for a salad?" Geordi whispered to Jenny.

"This is quite . . . astonishing, Captain," Picard said, exchanging a quick glance with Riker. "None of us has ever encountered anything quite like it. I'm most eager to begin."

Sejanus smiled. "We don't stand on ceremony, Captain, unlike our ancestors. Please."

Picard smiled in return, picked up the silver spoon beside the bowl, and filled his mouth with pickled hummingbird tongues and liquamen. He could scarcely taste the meat. It was overwhelmed by the sauce, which tasted salty, fishy, and cheesy all at once.

He forced a still-wider smile. "Superb!"

Sejanus grinned. "For non-Romans, it's something of an acquired taste! Here's how we do it." Eschewing his own spoon, he picked the bowl up with both hands and drained it in one long swallow. The other Magna Romans followed suit.

Picard took a deep breath and copied Sejanus.

Encouraged and relieved, his crew members did the same. Jenny swallowed the appetizer—and was surprised to find the dish remarkably similar to one of her homeworld's own delicacies.

She turned and spoke to Gaius Aldus, on her right, "This is wonderful!"

Gaius' serious face relaxed. "Thank you, Ensign. Non-Romans don't always react that way." He indicated Geordi, on Jenny's left, whose face had taken on a distinctly greenish pallor.

Jenny smothered a laugh as servitors appeared to take away the empty bowls and bring the next course. To her considerable surprise, they were all scantily clad young women.

"Not quite . . . standard Starfleet uniform, is it?" she asked Gaius.

The Magna Roman flushed slightly. "These aren't members of Starfleet. They're civilian employees, hired directly by the government of Magna Roma to work aboard our ships. Most of them are descendants of the slave class from imperial days." He shook his head. "I'm afraid the old social divisions still exist, even though they are no longer official. Seventy years is not sufficient to completely change a society that was based on slavery for thousands of years."

Jenny grimaced in distaste, and Gaius added quickly, "But we are trying."

"Yes. And I can see that it must be difficult. But you're still holding on to some things. Your uniform, for example."

"Strictly ceremonial, Ensign. And this"—Gaius slapped his metal breastplate proudly—"has nothing to do with slavery. This uniform is the part of our heritage we have a right to be proud of."

Jenny chewed that over thoughtfully. Clearly there was something to be said for the Roman attitude— the ship had fought brilliantly against great odds, and its captain seemed to her the epitome of strong leadership. Much of their attitude was surely the nature of the individuals involved. But she wondered if some of it—perhaps a great part of it—was in fact an element of Magna Roma's remarkable heritage.

Gaius said, "Ensign . . . or may I call you Jenny?"

"Oh, yes. Please do."

Gaius nodded, smiling. "In ancient times, we learned from the Graeci—the Greeks, you would say—to admire heroes and personal honor and all the other warrior virtues. We also learned from them to value learning itself, for its own sake, even though we lack their gift for theory. And we absorbed their admiration of health and physical beauty." He nodded toward the archway where the young women had exited.

Through it came four muscular young men wearing

simple tunics and carrying at shoulder height a huge metal platter upon which lay a roasted pig swimming in gravy. Steam rose from the carcass.

"We, however, taught the Graeci about food," Gaius Aldus added with a chuckle.

The young men placed the platter on the tiled floor, where it covered up much of the battle scene. One of them produced a long knife from somewhere and bent down.

Sejanus jumped to his feet. "Look at this, Captain Picard!" He was grinning in anticipated delight.

Jenny watched as the young man inserted the knife between the pig's shoulders, at the base of its neck, pushed it a short distance into the body, and then began to draw the knife downward toward the rump. She realized that the ribs must already have been severed to make it possible for him to do this with such ease. When he had completed his cut, he drew out the knife, and then he and his three companions gripped the edges of the cut with both hands and, at a nod from the one who had used the knife, pulled quickly and powerfully, spreading the pig's body open.

Exposed within were innumerable small, motionless birds floating in the gravy.

Sejanus had been watching Picard for his reaction.

"Thrushes!" the Roman said happily. "Live thrushes! See?" He realized something was wrong and turned back to the dead pig.

"What . . . ?"

"I'm afraid the birds have drowned in the sauce, sir," one of the young servitors said nervously.

Sejanus' jaw tightened. "Who's responsible for this?" He hissed the words between clenched teeth. The four young men turned pale and began to back away.

Gaius Aldus, also standing, reached out quickly and placed his hand on his captain's arm. "Didn't the ancients say, Lucius Aelius, that a fowl killed by drowning in wine has a particularly fine flavor?"

The guests from the *Enterprise* reacted with horror to this, but it seemed to soothe Sejanus. He smiled at his aide. "Right as always, Gaius." The four young servitors took the opportunity to scuttle out of the room. Sejanus ignored them and turned to Picard. "This man, Captain," he said, indicating Gaius Aldus, "is a treasure. He is my friend as well as my aide and first officer. He has served my family well and faithfully all of his life. He has been by my side since we were both children, guarding my honor as competently as he guards my life. He is *Magister Navis*— master of my ship, navigator, guide. This is very much a Magna Roman tradition."

"But the term is yet another parallel between your world and Earth, Captain Sejanus," Picard said as the company relaxed and sat down once again. The young women advanced and began carving the roast pig. "I believe the Romans of ancient Earth used it as well."

"Quite correct, Captain Picard," Sejanus said. "Your reputation does not do you justice, I see. You're a scholar *and* an officer."

"The similarities between Magna Roman and Earth history are uncanny—beyond even what Hodgkins'

Theory of parallel planetary development would predict," Commander Riker added.

"Only up to a certain point," Sejanus said. "From there, our planets followed radically different paths."

Data nodded. "On Earth the empire fell—and its dissolution led first to cultural fragmentation and the Dark Ages—"

"While on our world, the empire flourished and was able to lead Magna Roma to new levels of prosperity." This interruption came from Marcus Julius Volcinius —who had remained silent and almost antisocial up until now. He spoke in a patronizing voice, as if what he was saying was so obvious as to be barely worth mentioning.

"I do not believe all Magna Romans would agree with your statement, Lieutenant," Data said. "The brutal dictatorship that existed on your planet until recently was certainly not prosperous for the great majority of your citizens—"

"Prosperity is not measured strictly in terms of money," Marcus Julius Volcinius said, cutting off Data. "Culture, stability, peace—those are the things the great Magna Roman Empire brought to our world," the officer said, coming as close to sneering as he could without visibly looking down his nose at Data. "I would not expect a machine to understand such things."

To her left, Jenny saw Geordi visibly tense in his chair.

"Data," the engineer said in a clipped, tense voice, "is not a machine, Lieutenant."

"Yes I am, Geordi," Data said.

Sejanus laughed. "Gentlemen, please! I like to think we Magna Romans took the best traditions from both worlds—those of our native culture and those of Starfleet, shown to us when the Federation visited Magna Roma decades ago."

"One of the ships that first came to your world," Jenny said, "was also named the *Enterprise*—the name our ship carries as well."

Sejanus nodded. "Preserving the names of noble men and noble ships of the past is a fine tradition. I myself am named after a great man in our history— our greatest leader, in my opinion."

Data said, "On Earth, Lucius Aelius Sejanus was a monster who tried to overthrow the Emperor Tiberius but was exposed. He was imprisoned and then strangled in his cell, presumably upon Tiberius' orders, after which his body was given to the Roman mob, which tore it to pieces."

Gaius shuddered in his seat, as if what Data was describing was happening to Captain Sejanus.

"You see, Lieutenant, that is the precise point where the history of our two worlds parted company," the *Centurion*'s captain said. "On our world, Sejanus succeeded. He had the mad old Emperor Tiberius murdered and made himself emperor in his place. A cruel act, but one necessary to save Rome. Sejanus continued the cleansing by killing off all of the old emperor's family. He drove out the Christians and the other foreign religions and strengthened the old gods once again, thus strengthening Rome."

"And the dictatorship," Data said.

"And the dictatorship," Sejanus conceded. "But surely that's enough of politics for now." He snapped his fingers, and the servitors sprang forward. "Especially when there is food such as this to be enjoyed."

The young women began carving energetically, placing huge portions of meat on each guest's plate. As they served, other young women hurried into the room, bearing pitchers from which they poured generous helpings of dark red wine.

When all had been served, Marcus Julius Volcinius stood and raised his glass. All of the Magna Romans stood as well. Picard gestured to his officers, and they followed suit. "To Lucius Aelius Sejanus," Marcus said loudly. "To the Senate and the people of Magna Roma. And to victory." He and the other Romans drank deeply.

After a moment of hesitation, Picard sipped his wine. His officers immediately did the same. Then Picard spoke quickly, before the Romans could sit. "To the United Federation of Planets and democracy. And to peace."

There was an awkward moment of silence. Then Sejanus chuckled and drained his glass.

With that, the ice seemed to be broken. The conversation became general and convivial, and the Magna Romans and their guests ate and drank with enthusiasm.

But Gaius Aldus had noted Jenny's distaste of Marcus Volcinius. "You don't like him, do you?"

Turning in surprise, she replied, "I must learn to hide my feelings better."

Gaius smiled, "No need. He's a blustering fool and

no one of significance. As a diplomatic attaché, he has no real qualifications, but he *is* Captain Sejanus' cousin—a distasteful example of nepotism."

"Another archaic tradition that you still cling to?" Jenny countered.

Gaius flashed a smile. "As I said, we are trying."

Jenny returned his smile. "Tell me about your defeat of the M'dok. You were severely outgunned."

"We let their own arrogance defeat them. Using temporary power sinks to simulate battle damage, we drew them in close enough to destroy them."

"Your idea?" she asked.

"A technique I developed," he answered with pride in his voice.

"But was a death blow necessary? Could you take no survivors? They would have been a valuable—"

"Survivors?" Gaius' disbelief was plain on his face. "Lieutenant, we were at war. Would you take the time to judge whether or not your blow was a crippling one? And risk the lives of your own crew?"

Taken aback, Jenny replied, "I only suggested the possibility—"

"We were attacked!" Color rushed into Gaius' face as he brought his hand down on the table.

Jenny stared at him in open-mouthed surprise.

Gaius took a sip of wine and composed himself for a moment. "I must apologize for my outburst. I have served with Captain Sejanus my whole life. He and the crew of the *Centurion* have become my family, I have no other." He managed a slight smile. "I'm afraid that I can promise no leniency to anyone who raises a hand to them."

Jenny returned his steady gaze. "Then I admire your loyalty."

"I suspect it's a quality that you share," Gaius said.

Before Jenny could respond, her attention was drawn by the rather loud voice of Marcus Julius Volcinius across the table. He was gesturing with a greasy, unidentifiable bone and saying to the table at large, or perhaps to the entire room, "Now, take these Tenarans. They're just too decentralized. There's no authority, no one person in charge we can talk to. So they're easy prey for such fierce creatures as the M'dok. The *Centurion* can't stay here forever, can it, now, Captain Picard? No, of course not," he rushed on, answering his own question. Like many of the other Magna Romans, Marcus was growing flushed, his eyes overbright.

Picard, who had sipped his wine all evening, looked disapproving.

Sejanus' cousin's words had been clear and unslurred, Jenny observed, almost as if they had been thought out carefully beforehand. She wondered . . .

"Nor can the Federation afford to keep ships here indefinitely, defending a people who are unable to defend themselves," Marcus went on. "Their very organization—or lack of organization, I should say—makes it impossible for them to organize in their own defense. The gods help those who help themselves. So do Magni Romani."

True enough, Jenny thought, that part about defending themselves. She was about to say so aloud, but then Commander Riker said part of it for her. "We can all agree about the problem, Lieutenant, but I don't see a simple solution. Tenara is now a member of the Federation and thus has every right to expect the Federation to protect it. Moreover, the Federation never dictates the governmental policy of its member worlds, only that each government respect and protect its citizens' rights. We have to deal with Tenara as it is, not as we wish it to be."

Marcus waved his hand in dismissal. "Yes, yes, of course, Commander. We're here to defend them and to rebuild their world. This is supposed to strengthen them against future attack, but I say that we have to do more for them. For their own sake, the Tenarans have to change. We should teach them, help them to change themselves so that they can provide for their own defense. Romans have always been good at organization, and at teaching it."

"Usually," Data said calmly, "through conquest. Hardly an acceptable option in Tenara's case, sir."

Sejanus now broke into the conversation. "Agreed, Lieutenant. But we do have another choice."

"Which is?" Picard asked.

"Change the M'dok," Jenny blurted out.

All heads at the table turned to look at her.

"Hear, hear," Gaius said, smiling at her. "If the M'dok will not keep to the treaty voluntarily, we must force them to."

Geordi shook his head. "You're talking about war, Lieutenant."

"And what do we have now on Tenara?" Sejanus asked.

"We have a situation we must try to resolve," Picard said sharply. "We do not have war."

All at once the room fell silent as the two captains continued staring at each other.

The communicator on Picard's chest beeped once, shattering the quiet. "Excuse me, Captain," Picard said to Sejanus. He touched his chest. "Picard here."

The voice that came from the communicator was unmistakable.

"Lieutenant Worf, sir. We've just received an urgent message from Starfleet Command."

"Thank you, Lieutenant." Picard turned to Sejanus. "Forgive me, Captain, but it seems we must return to our ship immediately."

"Of course, of course," Sejanus said quickly. "Duty must come first. We can complete our discussions at some other time."

Picard nodded. He touched his chest again. *"Enterprise.* Transporter room. This is the captain. Six to beam back from the *Centurion,* immediately."

Chapter Two

"LET'S HEAR THAT MESSAGE, Mr. Worf," Picard said. The captain and his staff officers were all back on the bridge. Jenny de Luz had taken up a position behind Worf on the upper deck, at the mission operations station.

"Aye, sir. Audio only, on speakers now."

The voice was strong and self-assured, the voice of a man used to getting his way.

"Captain Picard, this is Admiral Howard Delapore. Starfleet Command has determined that the situation at Tenara is critical. The *Enterprise* is hereby ordered to stay within the system and to help the *Centurion* defend Tenara. Don't let *anyone* in. This applies to the entire Tenaran planetary system. From now on, only the space beyond the orbit of the outermost planet of the system is to be considered unclaimed territory. You are authorized to do whatever the situation requires in order to defend the system itself." Delapore's voice lowered. "I want you to understand how important that is, Picard. Command is placing a very high priority on this mission. You and Sejanus are two of the best we have, as are your ships and your crews. Good luck. Delapore out."

"That's all, sir," Worf said. "A second, coded message is attached, for your eyes only."

"Thank you, Lieutenant," Picard replied.

"Delapore?" At the engineering station next to Jenny, Geordi groaned, so softly only she could hear him.

"Closing off the system—aren't we risking war, sir?" Riker asked. "Given what you told us during your briefing."

Picard sighed. "We're certainly a step closer to it than we were before."

"I remember Delapore from the Academy." Riker smiled slightly. "A no-nonsense type."

"We had another name for him," Geordi said. "Old Iron—"

"I think we've all heard that name before, Lieutenant," Picard said sharply. "There's no need to repeat it."

"Yes, sir," Geordi said. "Sorry."

Jenny remembered Admiral Delapore (and his nickname) from the Academy. He was one of the senior instructors, a stocky gray-haired man who made it clear that he considered himself a man of action, one who preferred military missions to exploratory or diplomatic ones. *Now,* Jenny thought, *he has a military situation to deal with, and he's thriving on it.*

"Sir," Worf said. "Captain Sejanus is calling from the *Centurion.* He wants to know if we'll be rejoining him for the rest of the banquet."

He wants to know what was in the message from Starfleet Command, Jenny thought.

Sejanus' face filled the viewscreen. He was calling from the banquet hall; behind him, the dinner was still in full swing.

"Captain Picard," he said, his voice deep and grave, "I hope there's no trouble."

Picard responded instinctively. "No immediate trouble, Captain. It seems we've been ordered to remain here on Tenara and assist you in your defense of the planet."

Sejanus froze for a second. Then the Magna Roman relaxed and smiled.

"I don't see that there's a military necessity for that, Captain Picard, but Starfleet is, of course, subject to Federation Council control. Politics must be taken into account." He nodded in understanding. "Of course, we're glad to have you aboard. I have a briefing set up tomorrow with my crew, and then a meeting with the planetary council. Perhaps you could join us."

"Of course, Captain."

"Good. Then will you rejoin us now, Captain Picard? The evening is still young, and the feast far from over."

"I think not, Captain." Picard affected a smile of resignation. "I need some time to review the situation."

"As you wish. I'll have one of my men return your shuttlecraft." Sejanus bowed slightly. "Until tomorrow, then, Captain Picard."

"Until tomorrow, Captain Sejanus."

As the transmission ended, the viewscreen resumed its display of the stars and the *Centurion*.

Picard stood. "I suggest we all turn in. I suspect tomorrow is going to be a long, difficult day."

"Aye, sir," Riker said. "Data, you have the conn."

Jenny began following the two officers to the turbolift.

"One moment, Ensign," Worf said.

She turned.

"As my presence will be required aboard ship for the duration of the mission," Worf said, "I would like you to supervise all planetside security arrangements."

"Yes, sir," Jenny said. "Thank you, sir."

"I suggest you prepare yourself by reviewing the appropriate sections of the Starfleet manual," Worf added. He turned to the mission operations console and called up a portion of the text. "For instance, you will see here . . ."

Jenny sighed, and began reading over the Klingon's shoulder.

The libraries of a Federation starship are, without exception, extremely well-stocked. A device somewhat smaller than a human thumbnail can hold a quantity of information several times greater than all that which was contained in the Library of Alexandria. A much tinier device can process this information and quickly provide it for absorption by a human operator.

Marcus Julius Volcinius served as cultural attaché on special assignment to the *Centurion*. An intelligent, determined, and (by virtue of being the scion of one of the most patrician families of Magna Roma) very well-educated young man, he liked to think that he could absorb quite a bit of information.

He had left the banquet scarcely an hour ago, bored with the endless drinking and pointless banter. Besides, all the talk about changing the Tenarans, and Magna Roman tradition, had given him an idea.

"Computer."

"Working."

Machines, he thought with satisfaction, could always be relied upon to keep their place, never to overstep their bounds.

Except that walking computer, Data.

"Computer, tell me about the spread of the English language on Earth."

If there was a pause, Marcus couldn't detect it.

"English is the descendant of multiple languages: principally Anglo-Saxon, Latin, and various Celtic tongues. It was the primary language of England, one of three nations on a small island in the North Atlantic Ocean. In an ongoing process of colonial expansion beginning late in the sixteenth century and continuing until the early twentieth century, England established herself as the supreme political, military, and economic power in the world.

"With the expansion of English power, the language spread as well, eventually becoming the universal language of trade, science, and international politics.

By nature a dynamic and flexible language, it provides the basis of current Federation Standard, continuing to adapt to new words, new concepts, and new cultures."

It was obviously a capsule lecture, probably quoted verbatim from a statement made by some university professor, and it did not tell Marcus everything he wanted to know. He thought for a bit, and then asked, "Did the English make any deliberate efforts to hasten the spread of their language?"

"It is generally accepted," the computer said, "that the spread of the language was a natural and inevitable result of English economic dominance."

"And their culture spread similarly with the language?"

"Modes of dress, mores, methods of education and socialization, and most other cultural characteristics were based on an English standard all over Earth by the end of the twentieth century. It is generally accepted that popular entertainment had an enormous impact, particularly after the invention of television."

"But it took centuries," Marcus said, thinking aloud.

"Correct," the computer said.

Marcus gave the terminal an annoyed glance. His mind returned to the problem, but this time he kept his thoughts to himself. *It took the English centuries on Earth, but I only have weeks.*

"During the early days, when the spread of English was due to economic and military power, not popular education, didn't the various native peoples resent this invasion of an alien culture and try to indoctrinate their young against it?"

"On the contrary," the computer replied. "The English people were able to convince others of the superiority and prestige of an education obtained in an English-speaking country, and so the native populations eagerly sent their young to school in English institutions, where they absorbed both language and culture. The students then returned home to spread what they had learned."

Marcus sat back, drumming his fingers on the desktop. Conquest was not an option, in the words of his cousin.

But there was conquest as the warrior Sejanus understood it . . . and then again, there was conquest of an altogether different kind.

A kind of conquest that Marcus himself might be better qualified to undertake than Lucius Sejanus—or Jean-Luc Picard.

The *Centurion* briefing room the following morning was crowded. Unlike the banquet hall where Sejanus had first greeted the officers from the *Enterprise,* this room was organized with function rather than form in mind. Instead of purple curtains, the viewscreen was set into the naked wall; instead of Roman artwork, holographic charts and maps lined the walls.

Sejanus and Picard were seated at opposite ends of the long table in the center of the room, the senior officers from both ships between them. As everyone found a seat, Sejanus gestured sharply, and the view of Tenara that had filled the viewscreen was replaced with a lengthy organizational chart. All the officers had before them small personal viewers, which showed the same chart.

"I assume you have all been briefed?" Sejanus asked the *Enterprise* personnel.

Jenny de Luz joined in the general sounds of assent. Thanks to the extensive preparation she'd received from Lieutenant Worf, she felt she now knew more about Tenara than about her homeworld of Meramar.

"Then let us proceed to the business at hand," Sejanus said. "On your viewers is a governmental organization chart given to me by Melkinat, their planetary chairman. Now, as I'm sure you're all aware, the Tenaran government is notably decentralized. Their system of *saavtas* is quite primitive, and is actually a descendant of the council of tribal elders found in almost all precivilized societies. Unfortunately, their attempt to apply this system on a planetary scale has led not only to the lack of any strong central government but also to a very complex system of interlocking obligations and levels of authority."

But not more complex than Meramar, Jenny thought, studying the chart. On her feudal homeworld, her father had owed varying degrees of allegiance to three separate men, all of whom had had their own obligations to many others—one of whom had been one of her father's vassals! The hierarchy of Tenaran *saavtas* was relatively simple by contrast, with each *saavta* electing some of its members to the next most important *saavta*—all the way from the village *saavta* up to the planetary Great *Saavta*.

"But I stress," Sejanus continued, "that this is the framework within which we must operate. As I understand it, Starfleet has chosen us for a twofold mission: in the short term, to defend the Tenarans against future attack, and in the long term, to strengthen them so that they will be able to defend themselves in the future. Am I correct, Captain Picard?"

Picard nodded. "Absolutely. Starfleet Command has ordered both the *Centurion* and the *Enterprise* to assist the Tenarans—in whatever way possible. We must begin work immediately, to help them strengthen their economic and agricultural base, to bring them advanced medical care. We'll contribute all forms of training and resources at our disposal."

"What about their more immediate need, sir?" Gaius Aldus asked. "That of military assistance?"

Jenny nodded in agreement. It seemed clear to her that unless they could provide the Tenarans with some basic degree of security, all the other assistance would be meaningless.

Sejanus smiled. "We will begin training the Tenarans at once in basic combat techniques—"

"Excuse me, Captain Sejanus, but haven't the Tenarans been opposed to such training in the past?" Riker asked.

Jenny frowned. That piece of information hadn't been in the records she'd been studying.

"They have, Commander, but their leaders have requested it nevertheless," Sejanus said. "And it is something we must be prepared to provide, given the brutal nature of the M'dok attacks."

Captain Picard shifted uncomfortably in his chair.

"I must admit that I am troubled by this whole situation, Captain Sejanus," he said. "If we only knew why the M'dok were attacking now—"

Marcus Julius Volcinius, who was leaning against the entranceway to the briefing room, snorted in disgust.

"They are animals, Captain Picard. Why bother trying to understand their motivations?"

"They are sentient beings," Picard said firmly, glaring at the *Centurion*'s cultural attaché. "And there are reasons behind their actions, I'm sure. Mr. Data, have you been able to obtain any other information about what's happening within the M'dok Empire?"

The android shook his head. "Nothing definitive, sir. One rather obscure trade journal indicates that over the last few months there has been a marked increase in the importation of several drugs within the empire—"

"Drugs?" Picard asked. "What kind of drugs?"

"Mainly certain growth hormones, and their chemical analogues, sir."

"What *possible* significance could that have?" Marcus asked contemptuously, drawing out every syllable.

"I do not have sufficient information to conjecture at this point, Lieutenant," Data said. "However, I am expecting further information from Starfleet Command."

"We await that information," Sejanus said. "In the meantime, we must begin organizing the defense of Tenara."

Picard sighed heavily and exchanged a look of concern with his first officer. "I would prefer not to take such action without speaking to the planet's chairman first, Captain."

"His wishes seem quite clear to me, Captain, but . . ." Sejanus shrugged. "As you wish. We are scheduled to meet with Chairman Melkinat in two hours." The *Centurion*'s captain pressed his hands flat on the conference table and rose from his chair. "I will see you on the planet's surface, Captain."

Chapter Three

MELKINAT, Chairman of the Central Council of the Great *Saavta,* Most Honorable and Democratic Among the People of Tenara, and the nominal leader of that planet, was in no way prepared to meet with Captain Picard and Captain Sejanus, or to do much of anything else.

He was scared. Nothing in his comparatively uneventful life had prepared him to deal with such fear as he felt now.

The story Quillen had just told him . . .

Melkinat shook his head, trying to brush those horrible memories away. He had devoted his life to the people of Tenara, to the *saavtas.* As chairman of the Central Council, he stood for something honorable and decent, for individual freedom and dignity, for the principle that no man should rule over other men, and the idea that all people should make their own decisions so long as they did not interfere with the rights of others.

But against these things that are attacking us, these cat-monsters that call themselves M'dok, such noble principles mean nothing.

Tenarans had fought, he knew that. Centuries before, his people had been lifted from a world which, it was fairly certain now, had been Earth, but well before anyone on that planet had achieved the crudest aircraft, much less space travel.

From there they had been placed on Tenara, which was largely fertile prairie and glittering sea from pole to pole. With no enemies, no one to fight, they had exploded across the planetary surface. Plentiful territory and resources had made fighting practically unnecessary.

From their common cultural heritage and spirit of peaceful coexistence, the Tenarans had developed the basis of their present governmental system. When would-be conquerors had arisen, they had found the task of tearing apart the social fabric of the planet too great for even the most power-mad among them.

All this Melkinat knew, as a man knows his own name. He looked to the opposite wall of his small office, where a great ax hung on sturdy pegs. Perhaps it had been intended for chopping down trees, but notches along the edge and a few dark stains in those notches showed that it had once been used for a grimmer purpose.

It's an effort to find weapons like that on Tenara, Melkinat thought angrily, *not like on other worlds. We've had few wars, but never on a large scale. We want only peace and freedom. Why can't others respect that?*

He didn't know the answer to that, nor did he know the reason for the horrible attacks by the M'dok.

Which was why Tenara had requested help from the Federation.

Part of him wished the starships and their captains would go away. He saw their technology, their wonders, and felt that if he even allowed them to beam down to the planet with their weapons, it would somehow change his world irrevocably from the paradise it had been for so long.

Yet what choice did he have?

To be honest, a part of him was excited at the prospect of receiving help from the Federation, at tapping the shared knowledge of a thousand worlds.

What must it be like, he wondered, *to have done what both of these starship captains have done, to have seen so much, to have done so much? And what do they think of me, a man who has spent his whole life on one small world, who has accomplished so little?*

"Father?"

He looked up to see his daughter Gretna, who stood waiting in the doorway, hands on hips. She was dressed in sandals, shorts, and a colorful blouse, and he was struck again by how quickly she had grown—and how beautiful she had become.

"One of the starship captains has arrived already," she said.

"Thank you, daughter," he said, rising. At least he had one substantial accomplishment to his credit: Gretna, who showed every sign of succeeding him once his days as chairman were done. Surely neither starship captain could boast of offspring such as his. "We don't want to keep the Federation waiting, do we?"

"That's ground we've been over before, Father," Gretna said. "At this point, the answer is no."

Melkinat sighed. His daughter, though she understood why they needed the Federation's help, was even more reluctant than he to allow their weapons on Tenara.

He took her arm and strode out to meet the starship captain.

Captain Jean-Luc Picard tugged at his dress uniform to smooth out a minuscule wrinkle. Appearances were important in his work, and this would be his and Sejanus' first face-to-face meeting with the Tenaran leadership, but even so there was a limit to how far Picard was willing to go with all of this. He looked at himself in his mirror and decided that enough was enough.

He slapped his communicator. "Bridge."

"Lieutenant Commander Data here."

"Mr. Data, please inform Captain Sejanus that I'm ready to beam down, and then contact the Central Council of the Great *Saavta* and confirm that I'm on my way to the meeting."

Data replied, "Sir, we've just had a communication from Captain Sejanus. He's already on the planet surface. He sounded . . . troubled."

Picard felt the hair prickle along the back of his neck. "An emergency?"

The android hesitated. "He did not so specify, sir. Certainly we have detected no sign of any further attacks against Tenara."

"Hmm. All right, Data. Contact Captain Sejanus and tell him I'm on my way to the transporter room."

Picard closed that channel and opened another.

"Number One."

"Here, sir."

"Captain Sejanus has already beamed down, and it sounds like there are added complications. Can you join me in the transporter room?"

"I'm on my way, sir."

Picard's first officer was true to his word, arriving just as the captain was stepping up onto the transporter platform. Riker followed suit, and the captain nodded his readiness to Chief O'Brien. Picard was frowning, and the frown was still there when they reformed on the surface of Tenara.

They materialized in an airy, many-columned chamber. Two people, a middle-aged man and a much younger woman, were there waiting for them.

"Captain Picard," the man said, stepping forward and extending his hand. "I'm Melkinat, Chairman of the Central Council. And this"—he indicated the young woman, who moved to his side—"is my daughter Gretna."

"It's an honor, sir," Captain Picard said. "May I present my first officer, Commander William Riker."

Riker shook hands, his eyes lingering for a moment on the young woman.

"I understand there is a further problem, Chairman," Picard said.

Melkinat nodded. "A young man from one of our more remote villages has just come to us with a terrible story. Captain Sejanus is with him now."

"Lead on, Chairman," Picard said.

"A moment, Commander," Melkinat said, holding up his hand. "The young man seems uncomfortable with more than two or three people at once at this time. If you could—"

"I understand, sir," Riker said. "I'll wait out here."

"Perhaps you'll let me show you some of our planet, Commander," Gretna said.

Riker looked questioningly at his captain.

"It's all right, Number One," Picard said. "I'll brief you later."

"Aye, sir." Riker turned to Gretna and smiled. "Then I'll be happy to take a tour."

The two disappeared down one passageway, while Picard followed Melkinat down another. The chairman led him into a smaller room just off the Central Council chamber, where Sejanus and a young man Picard did not recognize were waiting. The Magna Roman was clearly upset, striding back and forth impatiently, muttering to himself.

By contrast, the young Tenaran was silent, and looked to Picard to be almost in a state of shock. He was sitting in the room's single chair, a typically light and graceful piece of Tenaran furniture that looked too fragile to bear the weight of a grown human. But the young man who sat in it was big-boned and heavily muscled, and the chair held up under him quite well.

"This is Quillen," Melkinat said.

Picard turned his attention to the young man.

Normally Quillen would have been an impressive physical specimen, but not now. He was pale and sweating as he chewed on his lower lip and pressed himself back into the chair.

Melkinat spoke to him soothingly. "This is Captain

Picard, Quillen. From the *Enterprise*. You know you can trust him. He's also from the Federation, just like Captain Sejanus—from Starfleet."

"We're here to help you," Picard added.

Quillen squirmed in his chair. "But I've already told you what happened!" He was whining and almost in tears. "Why can't *you* just tell him, and let me go home?"

Melkinat opened his mouth to say something, but Sejanus stepped forward abruptly and motioned him to silence. He leaned over Quillen, who shrank away from him. Sejanus stared at him until he met the Roman's eyes, and then Quillen seemed unable to look away. Sejanus said in a soft voice, "I want him to hear it from your mouth, Quillen, in your own words. I want Captain Picard to know what you experienced."

Quillen began to tremble.

Now Picard stepped forward, and Quillen turned toward him. Picard could see the terror in the young man's face, and he, too, spoke softly to him. "You may leave if you wish, Quillen. I'd like to hear your story from you. Captain Sejanus thinks I should, and I trust his judgment, but I've no wish to cause you pain."

Quillen relaxed slightly. "Th-thank you, Captain. I'll try, for the sake of my world." He took a deep breath, managed to stop himself from shaking, and began to tell his tale.

Quillen was a wood collector. In the communal economy of Tenaran village life, a few of the strongest young men were assigned the task of gathering the wood that the village needed for cooking and, in the colder weather, for heating. Much of what Quillen collected in the nearby forest was deadfall, which he carried back to the village on his shoulders. When the deadfall wasn't sufficient, he would search out old or dying or diseased trees and chop or saw them down. These, too, he would carry—or sometimes drag— back home.

He was an orphan, and was by nature a solitary person with no real friends, so this life-style suited him. Fond as he was of his village and most of his fellow villagers, Quillen loved roaming alone through the dappled sunlight of the forest most of all. He loved the sound of his ax and his saws as they cut through the trunks of trees, and he loved the smell of fresh-cut wood. He derived great pleasure from working his own powerful muscles as he carried great loads of wood home on his shoulders.

He liked the animals of the forest, large and small, and with the years they had grown to recognize him and no longer fled. "Sometimes," he said proudly to Picard, "they even stand around and watch me work. They're really interested, you see?"

Picard nodded. "I spent much time in the woods myself when I was young, Quillen. I understand your love for them." He thought of the holodeck program he had established to recreate an evergreen forest on the slopes of the Alps. "I find it can be a refuge from the complexities of dealing with other people."

The young Tenaran nodded vigorously. "Oh, yes, Captain!" A bit shamefacedly he added, "In fact, sometimes I put off going home for as long as I can, so that maybe it'll be late in the day and everyone in the village will be too tired to want to talk a lot to me. That's what happened that day. It was late when I got back. Too late . . ." He began to shake again.

It took some gentle prodding by Picard before Quillen was able to continue.

On his way home, Quillen often chose a pathway that took him up a small hill in the forest. The hilltop was bare because of a recent lightning-caused fire. If his load was a heavy one, he would circle the hill instead, but he liked standing atop it and looking out over the sea of treetops, undulating over hills and ridges like the waves of a real sea and stretching away to the horizon in all directions. Here and there, he could see clearings containing villages like his own. Last winter, the hilltop had been covered by a thin layer of frost that had crackled beneath his feet, and a few bushes that had survived the forest fire had been covered by ice, which glowed red in the setting sun.

He had been able to see smoke rising from chimneys to the south, marking his village.

But this spring evening, he had seen something different, something at first puzzling and then terrifying.

"Things flying around in the air over my village," he whispered. "At first I thought they were some strange kind of bird, but then I realized they looked a little bit like the flying machines that sometimes come to pick up the *saavta* members to take them to meetings at the regional capital. But there's usually only two or three of those, and this time there were a half-dozen. And they weren't landing. They were flying around in circles over the village. And then . . ." Tears began running down his cheeks.

And then white-hot beams lanced down from beneath the circling vehicles, and wherever the beams touched the ground, flames erupted. The vehicles were silent, the beams were silent, but even from that distance Quillen could hear the whoosh of the sudden fires, and the crackling of burning wood, and he thought he could hear human voices shouting and screaming.

Too shocked to think of the danger to himself, Quillen dropped his load of wood and his ax and saws and ran down the hill toward his village. His only thought was to save his fellow villagers.

Quillen ran along the forest track in the dimming light. He was blinded by tears, but his feet knew the way. Suddenly he felt the heat of a fire ahead and saw its glow shimmering through his tears. He stopped running and knuckled his eyes clear. The forest ahead of him was burning, blocking the path.

But he knew the woods here intimately, knew virtually every tree and bush, every gully, every creek, every mound of dirt. He left the trail and slipped through the forest, making his way around the fire and toward the village clearing by another route. It was that that saved his life.

Had he been able to stick to the trail, Quillen would have emerged into the clearing in plain sight, and then he would have faced the same fate as his fellow villagers.

Instead, he was still hidden in the trees at the edge

of the clearing, disguised by rapidly falling night and the dancing shadows cast by the huge fire raging in the center of the clearing.

The small, neat wooden houses were gone. In their place was an enormous bonfire. Around the fringes of the fire were the remnants of those few houses that had not been grouped with the others. They had been burned separately, reduced to collapsed piles of smoking embers, nothing still standing but their stone chimneys.

"But worst of all," Quillen whispered, "worst of all . . ."

His eyes stared into the remembered vision of horror.

Worst of all were the grotesque figures dancing around the fire in celebration. Big creatures, bigger than most men, with animal faces—pointed ears and terrible fangs glistening red in the firelight. They were covered with fur, and their arms and legs ended in heavily clawed paws.

"And they had tails," Quillen said. "Their tails kept twitching, sweeping back and forth over the ground. They reminded me of cats. Man-size cats. But they were wearing clothing—uniforms, it looked like to me."

Picard and Sejanus exchanged a glance. If they had needed more confirmation that the beings attacking Tenara were M'dok, then here it was.

But Quillen had more to tell them.

Now that he had managed to get himself to this point in his narrative, he had little trouble continuing.

He seemed compelled to press on with it, to purge himself of his awful memories and shift them over to these two strong, capable offworlders instead.

"I could see a lot of the villagers lying still on the ground, all over the clearing. They weren't moving at all. I don't think they were breathing. A lot more of them were still alive, but tied up. Some of them were unconscious, and some were awake, but they looked dazed. They weren't doing anything—not even struggling to get free. They had bruises, and some were bleeding from deep cuts on their backs."

The M'dok were yowling and screeching at each other. Quillen realized it was their speech. It sounded like a cat fight, he said, but the M'dok weren't fighting, and he realized that they were happy, that they were celebrating their victory.

They were swaggering around the clearing, and every now and then one of them would stalk over to the bound Tenarans, inspect them, and then walk away again looking satisfied.

Some of the M'dok had large chunks of meat impaled on long metal poles that they were roasting in the bonfire. Fat dripped from the meat and sizzled in the hot coals. When the meat was adequately charred, the M'dok drew it out, grabbed it with their paws, ignoring its heat, and tore mouthfuls off with their great sharp teeth.

The village had had a few cows and goats, used almost exclusively as dairy animals. It saddened Quillen to see them come to this pointless end. But then he saw how wrong his assumption was.

Two of the M'dok, wiping their greasy paws on their

uniforms, walked over to the bound Tenarans, se-
lected one, and grabbed him by the arms, one M'dok
on each side, and dragged him away toward the fire.
Quillen watched, more puzzled than alarmed.

One M'dok grabbed the Tenaran's head with a paw,
digging his claws into the man's scalp. The Tenaran
screamed and struggled, but the other M'dok joined
in to help, and the two powerful M'dok bent the
Tenaran's head back further and further. Quillen
closed his eyes, but he could hear the loud snap as the
villager's neck broke.

When he was able to make himself look again, the
M'dok had both drawn knives and were butchering
the Tenaran as though he were an animal. Only then
did Quillen realize where the chunks of roasted meat
had come from.

Quillen leaned against a tree, dazed and sickened.
Afraid to move at all for fear of drawing the M'dok's
attention, he stayed where he was until full night had
fallen. Then he backed slowly into the forest and
made his way in the dark, hands outstretched before
him. He stumbled deeper and deeper into the forest,
hoping that the M'dok were making so much noise
that they wouldn't hear the breaking twigs and whip-
ping branches as he passed through the forest.

Finally he collapsed, emotionally and physically
exhausted, and lay in a daze until morning.

With first light, Quillen roused himself and made
his way slowly, cautiously back toward his village.

The M'dok had left, taking the surviving Tenarans
with them. Nothing remained of the village in which

Quillen had grown up but smoking ruins. Nothing was left of the people he had known but a few scattered corpses and half-eaten pieces of roasted meat.

Quillen couldn't bear the sight of his village. He headed back into the sheltering, welcoming forest and lost himself there. He couldn't say how long he had wandered, trying to forget what he had seen.

The time came when, entirely by accident, he found himself in another village in a forest clearing. Later he learned that he had traveled almost three hundred kilometers from his starting point.

His first reaction was amazement that this village was thriving and whole—that it, too, had not been destroyed and its inhabitants eaten by catlike monsters. His second reaction was resentment that this place had survived while his own home had not. But his third reaction was a belated recognition of his duty to warn the Tenaran government about the attack.

Quillen entered the village and asked the first person he encountered to take him to the village *saavta*.

Quillen's voice trailed away. Picard could tell that the young man's strength was utterly used up.

"Word finally reached us here in Zhelnogra," Melkinat finished the story for Quillen, "and we had Quillen brought here."

He turned to Picard, and the anguish in his eyes was almost more than the *Enterprise*'s captain could bear.

"Now you see why we are in such desperate need of your assistance."

Before Picard could comment, Sejanus stepped forward and placed a hand on Melkinat's shoulder.

"You will have our assistance, Chairman— everything we can give you. No M'dok will reach the surface of Tenara again. I pledge my word."

"Thank you, Captain," Melkinat said.

Picard bit his lip. "Excuse me, Captain Sejanus, Chairman Melkinat."

Both men turned to look at him.

"I believe we need some time to consider this latest development, Captain," Picard said. "I suggest we pass along Quillen's story to Starfleet Command, and see if—"

"Am I to understand you do not favor giving us the weapons we need to defend ourselves?" Melkinat interrupted.

"I favor finding a peaceful solution to this problem, Chairman. Quillen's story has given us another piece to this puzzle. I suggest we may find its solution somewhat easier now."

Sejanus frowned. "I see your point, Picard. But we must prepare the Tenarans for the worst."

Melkinat shook his head sadly. "For the worst? What 'worst' could there possibly be?"

Picard said nothing, but somehow he doubted that the Tenarans understood the ultimate horrors of war.

William Riker tore his attention away from the pointing arm itself and looked where the girl was pointing. She had caught the motion of his eyes, and she smiled slightly in self-satisfaction.

"I see," Riker said. "Quite a complex, by any world's standards."

Gretna Melkinata laughed. "You're trying to flatter us, Commander. I realize how small and silly all of this must look, compared to what you've seen on the more advanced planets in the Federation."

"Will, please. That's what my friends call me." He smiled at Gretna, who blushed slightly and turned her attention back to the valley below them.

The valley was filling with water. Slowly but steadily, day after day, centimeter by centimeter, the level rose, creeping up the valley sides, covering trees and rocks and bushes forever. To their right, the river that was the water's source rushed into the valley through a narrow gorge. White water roared down a fall into a deep hole beneath it, and then flowed more peacefully down the valley. To the left, the far end of the valley, the river's outlet was blocked by the high white wall of a newly built dam.

At this point the surface of the new lake had not yet reached the spillway atop the dam. When it did, the water would drop down another fall—this one man-made. Eventually the dam would generate more electricity than all of the existing power stations on Tenara combined.

Even high up on the hillside, Riker could smell the spray from the waterfall. He breathed in deeply. "What a delightful place! It's beautiful here."

Gretna nodded. "I've been coming here since I was

a child. But now we're changing it forever," she said sadly. She shook the mood away. "Come on, Will. Let's get closer." She ran down the hillside.

Riker watched Gretna appreciatively for a moment before following her. It was summer now in Tenara's northern temperate zone, and he felt suddenly conspicuous and clumsy in his Starfleet uniform. He liked the way the Tenarans seemed to blend into their environment, and he admired their love of their world. Short as his visit on the surface had been so far, he had already absorbed enough of the Tenaran mindset to see how jarring the new dam was, how conspicuous and clumsy it looked. His appreciation of Gretna Melkinata went beyond such considerations, though; he was powerfully attracted to her.

Which is something that a career Starfleet officer should know better than to let happen, he told himself. *You'll probably be gone in a few days.* He shook his head in annoyance at himself and walked down the hillside in the mild sunlight.

When he reached her, Gretna was sitting on a low rock looking pensively downward at the lake. She pointed downward again. "Right under there, there used to be an old stone bridge over the river. When I was a child, my secret hiding place was under that bridge." She dropped her arm and smiled. "Where I used to go when I didn't want anyone to find me. Actually, I suspect my parents knew where I was, but they used to go along with the game and pretend not to know."

Such a gentle world, Riker thought. "Tenara will be

stronger with this new power supply," he said carefully. "Better able to protect itself, if that becomes necessary."

Gretna sighed. "Oh, I know that." She put her hands up and pulled her fingers through her shoulder-length blond hair—a nervous habit, but one Riker found charming. "But, Will, what will we be protecting? What's going to happen to Tenara in the process? And will it still be worth protecting?"

Riker winced. "Must we destroy all that's good in a society in order to save it from its enemies? That's a question the great philosophers of various worlds have struggled with for centuries, Gretna, and I don't feel qualified to deal with it."

Gretna turned and looked at him thoughtfully. "So you just put it out of your mind and follow orders."

"Of course not!" Riker made no attempt to hide how offended he was. "I swore an oath to uphold the principles of the Federation. I'm not expected to follow orders that violate those principles."

"The problem," Gretna pointed out, "is that principles tend to be vague and general, but orders are specific and deal with the immediate present."

"Yes," Riker said uncomfortably. "Dammit, Gretna, you're supposed to be a naive girl from a provincial planet."

She laughed, suddenly lighthearted. "And why should Tenara's lack of advanced technology make me naive, Commander Riker? People are born and die here too, just like anywhere else. They fall in love; they encounter happiness and sadness—in short, we're like sentients everywhere. Do you really find your assignment to Tenara so dull and unbearable, Commander?" She smiled and changed that to, "Will?"

Riker smiled back. "This is one of the most enticing worlds I've ever been on."

"And there's more to it than you've seen so far," Gretna said, looking directly at him.

Now it was Riker's turn to blush.

His communicator beeped.

"Riker here." He rose to his feet and unconsciously snapped to attention.

"This is Lieutenant Worf, Commander. Captain Picard and Captain Sejanus have beamed back from Tenara and called an emergency staff officers' meeting on the *Centurion.*"

"Understood," Riker said. He shrugged apologetically and said to Gretna, "I have to go."

She nodded. "I hope you'll find time to return."

"We've got to finish that tour, remember?"

"We do at that," she said, standing herself.

"Beam me directly to the *Centurion,* Lieutenant Worf," Riker said.

He allowed himself another brief smile at Gretna before the transporter beam took him.

When Picard finished telling the assembled officers Quillen's story, there was a moment of stunned silence.

Data was the first to break it.

"With this new information, sir, I believe I can now offer a reasonable conjecture for the M'dok's behavior," the android said. "It is highly likely that the drugs the M'dok have been importing—the growth hormones—were intended to increase the amount of sustenance available from the creatures the M'dok use as their food animals—"

Across the table from Data, Jenny grimaced.

"I can further postulate," the android continued, "that these attempts have failed, and thus the M'dok have turned elsewhere for sustenance."

"And Tenara just happens to be the closest world to the empire that qualifies," Riker said.

The android said, "There are of course many instances of such behavior in the history of all the civilized worlds. The ancestors of many of the crew members on this ship once ate their fellows. In the case of Tenara, the feeding is inter- rather than intraspecies, so our emotional reaction is not really justified. By definition, we are not talking about cannibalism."

"Commander," Picard said angrily, "the Tenarans are sentient humanoids, and so are the attackers. We've all advanced far enough to feel that all sentient humanoids are members of the same species."

Data had opened his mouth to protest, but thought better of it and said nothing.

"Why would their food herds suddenly fail to supply them?" Sejanus asked.

"A population explosion, a planetary catastrophe —there are any number of possibilities. Disease, however, remains the most likely one."

"Well," Picard said, "at least we know what we're up against now. Mr. Data, I'd like you to prepare a message to Starfleet Command advising them of the situation and suggesting that they initiate contact with the M'dok Empire to offer our assistance."

"And if they won't take that assistance, sir?" This question came from Gaius Aldus, who was again seated next to Jenny. "Isn't our first obligation to protect the Tenarans—no matter the cost in M'dok lives?"

Picard frowned in disapproval. "I would hope there's a way other than war to protect our citizens' lives, Lieutenant. Two hundred years ago, our own society was a more martial one. Our first war with the M'dok was particularly vicious and bloody, and a second war with them might be even worse. The loss of life on both sides would be unimaginable. Now that we know what they are doing here, we must try to help the M'dok—"

"Help them?" Marcus Volcinius asked, incredulous. "I cannot believe my ears, Captain. They have slaughtered innocent beings, eaten them as if they were cattle—and you want to help them?"

"I want to help them," Picard said angrily, "because I do not want this to happen again! What would you have me do, slaughter the M'dok in retaliation?"

Sejanus raised a hand to calm his cousin, and then spoke for the first time during the conference.

"I'm sorry, Captain. None of us wants this to happen again."

"Of course not," Picard said, managing a tight-lipped smile, "but we must not rush into confrontation with the M'dok. That would start us down a road we would find hard to turn back from."

"However, we must still begin the transport of

security personnel and defensive equipment to the surface immediately," Sejanus said. "So that when the M'dok strike next, they are not allowed to plunder the planet freely."

Picard shook his head in frustration. "I agree. I can see no other option at this time. Ensign de Luz will act as the *Enterprise*'s coordinator for all ground security matters."

"I will be performing that job for the *Centurion*," Gaius Aldus said, smiling at Jenny.

"There is one more thing I would like to say—to all of you," Picard began. He paused a moment for effect, and when he began speaking again, Jenny sensed his words were meant more for the crew of the *Centurion* than for his own officers. "I ask each one of you to remember what it is we are here to do. Tenara has asked for our help against the M'dok, but we must be sure that is all we give them. Neither Starfleet nor the Tenarans themselves desire a permanent Starfleet presence here; our goal must be to aid the Tenarans.

"We're not here for a war, after all. We're here to prevent one."

Chapter Four

THE FOLLOWING MORNING, security personnel from both starships began setting up defenses on Tenara.

Jenny de Luz supervised the team from the *Enterprise*, which went quietly and efficiently to work, establishing their camp and setting up perimeter security. They brought down no weapons heavier than phasers, intending to familiarize the Tenarans with these before bringing down the ground-based defenses.

In contrast, when the crew members from the *Centurion* landed a few hundred meters away, they spilled out and hit the ground in defensive positions in an elaborate show of force, maintaining their positions for several minutes, glaring out at the unoffending scenery. Then, at some unheard signal, they spread out their perimeter and started unloading weapons shocking in both quantity and type: phaser rifles, tripod-mounted phaser cannon, and other implements of mass destruction Jenny had thought long ago mothballed at Starfleet headquarters against the worst of eventualities.

She cheered up when she saw Gaius Aldus.

She saluted him casually as he approached; he returned her greeting with a technically perfect stiff-armed Roman salute.

"I'm a bit . . . surprised at the magnitude of your efforts, Commander," she said curiously, watching the Magni Romani work busily in squads of ten. That, too, she felt, should mean something to her.

"All is as our captains have ordered," he told her.

"Indeed . . ." She continued to look around. The *Centurion* crew worked with the well-drilled efficiency which she knew had marked the ancient Roman soldiers on Earth as well as soldiers from Gaius Aldus' planet. How natural it seems to think of the Magni Romani as soldiers instead of simply Starfleet personnel, she thought suddenly. They were setting up their heavy weapons in a well-planned, deadly order, capable of turning the surrounding area into several square kilometers of shattered rock and scorched dirt.

"But surely, Magister, it would have been better to bring down the equipment slowly, to let the Tenarans grow accustomed to it?" she asked.

"And if the worst happens? If the M'dok attack in force and manage to break past the starships to this planet?" Gaius shook his head. "We Romans can't abide defenselessness, Jenny. And by the way, when are you going to start calling me by my name? Even Romans aren't formal all the time."

She managed a small smile, but did not reply. She went on watching the activities of both the *Enterprise* and the *Centurion* personnel—and watching Gaius Aldus out of the corner of her eye.

She was less disturbed by the attraction she felt to

him as woman to man—that would have been no more than she expected, for he was pleasant and handsome—than by the kinship she sensed between them, soldier to soldier.

Meramar is a martial world, she reflected, *and I am a true child of that world. A knife was put into my hand as soon as my fingers were large enough to close around the handle. But I've turned my back on that for the Federation's sake, and replaced death with life. . . .*

Haven't I?

She forced the discomfiting thought away and said, "I notice that your people don't observe standard Starfleet work patterns."

Gaius' smile transformed his normally serious face, giving it an appealing warmth and charm.

"Ah, the tens, you mean," Gaius said. "Our ways worked so well for us, didn't they?" *Gave us dominion over our world.* "We're traditionalists in many areas. Warfare is one of them."

"But Starfleet requires that all of its people train in certain ways," Jenny began in protest.

"And we abide by those regulations," Gaius said promptly. He smiled again. "We Romans have also always been very good at following rules to the letter. However, we do train our people in the Roman way as well."

"If it works," Jenny said doubtfully, "then I suppose no one can object."

"Oh, yes, it works! Would you like to see how well it works?"

"How do you mean?"

"I often lead our men in training sessions on our

holodeck. I'd be happy to have you observe—or even participate, if you like."

The prospect seemed an echo of Jenny's own up-bringing, and for that very reason it both attracted and repelled her. The invitation seemed almost to be an offer of friendship, of closeness, that she wasn't yet ready for. She temporized by saying, "If I *were* to accept, I think I'd be more interested in participating than observing."

Gaius frowned uncertainly. "Too much for a non-Roman," he muttered. He looked her up and down carefully—an analytical look, weighing and balancing, nothing sexual in it. "Well, perhaps. Yes, I can see . . ." He broke off, blushing suddenly. "Forgive me. I wasn't thinking. You'd be welcome. In fact, we'd be honored to have you there."

So now the onus was on Jenny. *Too soon!* she thought, touched by panic. She had always reacted to strong overtures of friendship or affection by drawing back, and, unable to stop herself, she did so now. She said abruptly, "I'll let you know."

She turned away and walked rapidly back to the *Enterprise* personnel, leaving Gaius Aldus staring after her in surprise.

Far away from the Tenaran capital city, invasion of an entirely different kind was taking place.

On a hillside overlooking a bowl-shaped valley, Marcus Julius Volcinius paused to catch his breath. A creek meandered through the valley, whose floor and sides were covered with cultivated fields. To Marcus' eye, untutored in agrarian matters, the crop in those fields looked like what Magna Romans called *frumentum,* grown high and ready for harvesting. However, he realized that the plant might be something else entirely, something native to Tenara, and perhaps it was still at an early stage of its growth cycle. Such concerns were the province of farmers, not something an urban patrician concerned himself with.

It would help to know, though, he told himself, *in order to open the conversation with these peasants on a friendly level.*

Boots would have been impractical on such uneven ground, and armor out of the question in the warm sunlight. Marcus congratulated himself on having chosen sandals and a simple tunic. Dressed this way, he was very comfortable. As always, he was very pleased with himself.

Across the valley, a small village sat near the top of one of the hills. It was well above the limit of the cultivated fields, its houses set close together so that they didn't use up any of the arable land. Marcus nodded his approval of such efficiency. The village was his destination. He had beamed down just out of sight of it but within easy walking distance.

Marcus turned and set out across the brow of the hills that formed the sides of the valley. He could have saved quite a bit of time and distance by cutting across the valley, but that would have taken him through some of the cultivated land. Such peasants as these, Marcus knew, would be angered by any damage to their crops.

At least that was the way it was on Magna Roma these days. Spurred on by their initial contact with the Federation, the old Imperial Government had begun its sudden, yet surprisingly peaceful transformation into the Republic of today almost eighty years ago. Around the time of his birth, the new Magna Roman government had begun its serious push for land reform. The *latifundia,* the great estates of imperial days, had been broken up and parceled out to people whose ancestors had been serfs on those very *latifundia.* The descendants of the serfs now farmed their own land, and would not tolerate the presence of someone like Marcus on that land. Membership in the Volcinii *gens,* or any of the other great, ancient clans, had once ensured the terrified obedience of the serfs. Now it guaranteed only the hatred of their descendants.

In the valley, a swarm of people moved among the rows of plants, bent over, searching for weeds and pest damage. One of them noticed Marcus and called out to him. The others straightened and looked where their comrade was pointing. Still immersed in his gloomy thoughts of the current situation on his homeworld, Marcus stiffened in momentary fear of the farmers.

Then he realized that they were waving at him in normal Tenaran friendliness. He smiled broadly at them, waved back, and continued toward the village.

The village was empty, but the schoolhouse was easy to find.

Once he was in the village, Marcus could see that it consisted of houses arranged in a rough circle around a larger building, which he knew would be the combination meeting hall, *saavta* assembly hall, and school.

All of the houses were one-story square structures made of wood, with rounded roofs of roughly woven dried grass. It was a primitive design in Marcus' eyes, but he had to admit that it probably served well in the mild climate of these parts.

The central building, though, was two stories high, fronted by a ground-level porch. Marcus squinted upward and made out individual wooden planks, each carefully bent into a curve, so that together they formed the dome of the roof. *A lot of trouble to go to,* he thought. It graphically demonstrated how important this building was to the Tenarans. That pleased Marcus. It was a kinship. The Senate of Magna Roma still met in the very same stone building in the city of Rome that the ancient Romans had used, long before their empire had conquered their entire world. That building had an almost religious significance for Magna Romans, and here, in the care taken with the *saavta* building in this obscure village on Tenara, he saw the foundation of the same mystical respect. Marcus nodded approvingly and stepped onto the porch.

The ground floor consisted of one large room, quite empty. *Just like the village,* Marcus thought. All of the inhabitants must be down in the valley tending to their crops. Then he heard voices. To his right, he saw a flight of stairs. He climbed it to the second floor, moving a bit hesitantly, still unsure of his reception.

The second floor was divided into four rooms, only one of which was in use. A dozen children sat on the floor or on chairs, or leaned against the walls, listening with varying degrees of interest to an older woman in the center of the room.

Marcus stopped in the doorway, unobserved, and listened for a while. The woman was reciting a list of names in an almost singsong voice.

Names to learn by rote, Marcus thought scornfully. *Peasant lore, passed down orally to the next generation.*

He stepped forward and cleared his throat.

The teacher stopped in mid-word and looked at Marcus in confusion. "Yes? Who—"

But the children knew. Somehow, their grapevine had carried to them word of the exciting visitors from space. "He's from Starfleet!" one of them shouted, and then they all rushed at Marcus, grinning eagerly.

He was alarmed again for a moment, but held his ground and smiled at the children.

They surrounded him, fingering the machine-made cloth of his tunic with awe, and showering him with questions. He could hardly make out a word they were saying.

"One at a time," he laughed. "Please!"

The teacher's voice cut through the babble. "Children! Show some manners!" When their voices quieted, she said to Marcus, "Are you lost, sir? Can we help you find your way somewhere?"

Marcus grinned happily. *This is so easy!* "No, actually I'm right where I wanted to be. I'm here to help you teach."

"Help me teach?" she repeated in bewilderment.

"Oh, yes." He held up the small hand computer he

had brought with him from the *Centurion.* "With your permission, I thought I'd give your students a short course in Roman history."

The happy shouts of the children drowned out the teacher's confused protests and were all the encouragement Marcus needed. Tenara had a long way to go, and Marcus Julius Volcinius was here to guide it in the right direction.

The day's work had been long and physically exhausting. Jenny was glad when the last of the equipment was beamed down, and the temporary shelters for the *Enterprise* personnel set up.

Again, by way of contrast, the *Centurion's* personnel had beamed down prefabricated building blocks, which they quickly assembled into a barracks that resembled nothing so much as an armed fortress to Jenny, and (from the shocked expressions on their faces) to the group of Tenarans accompanying her.

This last part of Jenny's day was the most exhausting; not physically, but mentally. She was taking Chairman Melkinat and the other members of the Great *Saavta* on a brief tour of the ground-based defense installations the Magna Romans were setting up. There were about thirty of them altogether, walking behind her. Even as she spoke, pointing out each weapon and detailing its capabilities, she could sense the Tenarans' distaste and see the way they cringed from the machines she was showing them.

Commander Riker was right, she thought. *I don't think these people are ready for this.*

Jenny turned to them. "Look, I know you don't

really approve of all of this, but we're doing it to protect you from further M'dok attacks. If you really don't want any of these devices"—she swept her arm out to indicate the entire collection of weapons and the crews manning them—"you can just tell us to take them away and leave, and we will. This is your world, and we're only here by invitation."

She'd spoken perhaps more plainly than she'd intended—the Tenarans seemed to sense the annoyance in her voice and backed away from her.

Melkinat stepped forward from the pack and said gently, "Don't distress yourself on our account, Ensign de Luz. We all understand the need for these weapons, and we appreciate the efforts of your two ships to help us." He turned to the other Tenarans, who added their loud assurances to his.

The chairman continued, "Please don't misinterpret our distaste for disapproval, Ensign. It's just . . . well, difficult for us."

He drew a deep breath and pointed at the phaser-mounted cannon the *Centurion*'s crew had transported down. "These are very powerful devices. You say they can detect a ship in space as soon as it approaches Tenara, and if necessary, even destroy it while it's still in space. If that's so, then why do you—I mean, we—need any other installations than this one? I know you plan to place similar devices elsewhere on Tenara."

"Because of blind spots, sir," Jenny said. The Tenarans looked puzzled. "You see," she explained, "none of these weapons we have here can fire through a planet, so that means that an enemy—a raider, I should say—can approach in Tenara's shadow, in other words, from such a direction that the planet itself shields the ship from the weapons. This means that even though the satellite system we plan to set up can detect a raider approaching from any direction, the weapons may not be able to fire on it. So we plan—with your permission, of course—to establish similar collections of weapons across Tenara's land surfaces and on rafts out at sea, so that no matter which direction the M'dok try to approach from, they can still be kept away."

"All over the world?" one of the Tenarans repeated. This was an older woman, her hair pure white and thinning, who had earlier been introduced to Jenny as Anka. "I had hoped," Anka went on, "that we could limit the exposure of our people to these devices, but if they're everywhere, then that becomes impossible, doesn't it?"

"I suppose it's the price we have to pay to protect our world, Anka," Melkinat said sadly, his distress evident.

"The price is not worth paying, Chairman."

The loud grumblings that followed her words indicated that a great many of her fellow Tenarans agreed with her.

"We have been over this before," Melkinat said. "The vote was to defend our world—not to die like cattle."

Anka glared at him. "I call for another vote, then."

Jenny saw that the Tenarans had split into two factions—factions rapidly moving apart from each other. The smaller group consisted of Melkinat and the other members of the Central Council. The larger group, about two dozen people, included Anka and those Great *Saavta* members who were not part of the Central Council.

Jenny tried to defuse the situation. "Our presence here is a deterrent, one we hope will shortly become unnecessary. If we can convince the M'dok to stop these raids—"

"And if you can't?" A member of Anka's faction, a slender, bearded man with a surprisingly deep voice, moved to the front of the pack. "What then?"

"We have every hope that we will be able to." Jenny knew as soon as she spoke how weak her answer sounded.

"I have another question for you, Melkinat," Anka demanded. "What happens when the Federation leaves? Who will man these weapons then?"

The grumbling from the people behind her grew even louder.

Melkinat stepped in front of Jenny and stood face-to-face with Anka. To his credit, he did not try to dodge the issue. "If the Federation leaves, *we* will have to man the weapons."

"Never!" she said.

"It is that or perish," Melkinat said simply.

"Better to die with our principles intact than to become killers ourselves," Anka said.

"Anka's right!" Yet another member of the older woman's faction spoke up now. "These weapons must not stay here!"

Jenny shouted for quiet, but few of the Tenarans could hear her over their own noise. Several did turn their attention her way, though, their faces red and their fists raised.

Suddenly Jenny realized these peaceful people were just as capable of violence as anyone else. It was just a matter of finding the right trigger—and she seemed to have found it.

With outward calm she raised her hand slowly to the communicator contained in the insignia on her chest. But then she stopped. The Tenarans were looking at each other, trying to draw the courage to make the first irretrievable move. The air was electric with tension, with the potential of violence. Jenny feared that her call to the *Enterprise* to beam her up would trigger it. She might get hurt—or lose control and hurt some of the Tenarans.

And then came the familiar sound of a transporter. The open space around Jenny began to fill with gold-shirted security troops. The Tenarans scuttled backward.

Jenny sighed in relief and dropped her hand. *How did the* Enterprise *know I needed help?*

And then something odd struck her about this security force: in addition to the normal equipment, each one wore a short sword at his waist. *Why, they're Magna Romana! They aren't from the* Enterprise *at all. They're from the* Centurion.

A stocky figure pushed his way through the security cordon to her side. "Are you all right, Jenny?"

She laughed. "Just fine, Gaius. The Roman cavalry arrived in the nick of time."

Gaius Aldus smiled in return. "Romans have always believed in punctuality."

The Tenarans had retreated still further while Jenny and Gaius Aldus spoke. Now they were gathered in a group at a distance, acting like small children aware of their guilt. Melkinat approached the watchful Magna Roman force hesitantly.

"It's all right," Jenny called out. "Let them through."

The security forces parted, forming a corridor through which the two Tenarans walked nervously, their eyes flicking from side to side. Jenny waited for them without expression.

Melkinat licked his lips and said, "Ensign, I can't tell you how sorry I am that this happened."

"I know you are," Jenny said. "Melkinat, take your people back to Zhelnogra. I'm sure Captain Picard will be in contact with you."

Gaius Aldus gestured, and the security troops parted again for Melkinat to pass through.

Jenny and Gaius could see Melkinat talking to the other Tenarans earnestly. The group gestured frequently toward the Magna Roman security force, then broke up and headed back toward the handful of old ground vehicles into which they had crowded for the long trip from Zhelnogra. They jammed themselves back into the vehicles and began the trip home.

Jenny hesitated, then gestured for Gaius to walk a short distance away with her. When she was sure they were out of earshot of the others, she said to him, "Do you know what one of the Tenarans told me today?"

Gaius shook his head.

"There hasn't been a crime recorded on Tenara in three hundred years. Nothing—murder, robbery, and certainly not riot. And yet look what almost happened here."

Gaius shrugged. "Tenara was lucky. It was isolated from the rest of the Galaxy and hence from reality. The ancestors of these people came from Earth, just like yours did. They're no different from you genetically. They're not some superior life form. So now reality has appeared, and they're reacting to it in a normal human way."

Jenny shook her head impatiently. "That's not what I meant. You're right: their isolation is over, and they're going to have to pay a price for that. But that's not the inevitable result of contact with the rest of the Galaxy. There're plenty of worlds where it doesn't happen at all!"

Gaius smiled grimly. "Perhaps, not having tasted of it earlier, the Tenarans are unusually susceptible to violence."

Jenny shook her head again. "No! It's as if it's some sort of virus that we brought with us from the outside."

"You're wrong, Jenny," Gaius insisted. He looked at her face, noted the lines of weariness. "You're tired," he said gently. "You've been working nonstop all day. You need a rest."

Jenny managed a smile. "I think you're right about that."

The two were silent a moment.

Jenny was suddenly aware of her proximity to Gaius and turned to look at the sun setting over the valley. The sunsets she remembered from Meramar were unexceptional. Darkness came swiftly to the perpetually overcast sky, as if the sun were simply switched off.

Not so on Tenara, where the sun was dimming reluctantly and going out in a blaze of rich blues and purples. As Jenny watched, the purples turned to reds and golds, and she felt the cares of the last few hours leave her. For now, she was content to stand and watch the sun's last rays play out over the trees of the valley.

It almost looks like Paradise—except for the weapons we've brought down here.

As if he'd been reading her thoughts, Gaius spoke. "This is such a beautiful world. Why don't you go out and enjoy it?"

"I'd like to," Jenny said.

And then, before she could stop herself, she thought:

Before we change it forever.

Chapter Five

CAPTAIN JEAN-LUC PICARD studied the satellite pattern depicted on the screen before him. The web of satellites the *Enterprise* and *Centurion* had set up around Tenara over the last week was in strict compliance with Starfleet regulations, and a computer analysis of the resulting defense net had given the satellites another mark of approval.

Then why do I feel as if that is not enough?

He glanced again at the pattern of the satellites' orbits, examined the encryption of the carrier waves of their sensors, and pored over the mechanical stress readouts of their casings. But they told him nothing new.

Not for the first time in the last week, he wished someone other than Commander Riker had led the away team to Tenara. He valued all his staff officers, but missed his second-in-command's input at moments like these—when his instincts were at war with his training.

A soft beep sounded behind Picard.

"Incoming communication from the *Centurion,* sir," Worf said.

"On-screen."

The picture of the *Centurion,* about one hundred kilometers ahead of the *Enterprise,* vanished from the main viewscreen and was replaced by the stern features of Captain Sejanus.

"I have logged my approval of the satellite-detection net," Sejanus said. "If you will now add yours, Captain, our engineers can begin powering up the system."

"I would like to run one further safety check with my chief engineer, Captain," Picard said. "If it meets with his approval, we'll put the net on-line."

Sejanus frowned.

"I thought all safety checks had been completed, Picard," the *Centurion*'s captain said, a trace of impatience in his voice. "We need to have the system operating as soon as possible."

"We need to have the system operating *safely,* Captain," Picard said. "One more check."

"Your caution is commendable," Sejanus said, but he was clearly not pleased. "I leave it to you to bring the system on-line. *Centurion* out."

Picard opened a channel to engineering. "Mr. La Forge, how are we doing?"

"All set on this end, sir. Just give the word."

"Lieutenant Worf?" Picard asked, swiveling in his command chair.

Worf studied his console. "According to my readouts, the monitor system for the net is functioning perfectly."

"Naturally," Geordi said, his voice carrying a touch of amusement. "Did you expect any less?"

"Excellent work, Mr. La Forge," Picard said.

"I didn't do it all myself, Commander. The *Centurion* personnel had most of the basic system already designed."

"Of course." Picard nodded. Over the past few days, a team of engineers from the *Centurion* had been working with the *Enterprise* engineering personnel in the design and implementation of the satellite-detection net. And maybe that was the problem, he told himself. Maybe he just didn't trust the work the *Centurion* people were doing.

Ridiculous. He was letting the fact that he was personally uncomfortable with Captain Sejanus get in the way of his job.

"Congratulate them for me as well, Lieutenant," Picard said. "Begin powering up the satellite network."

"Right away, sir." Geordi hesitated a moment, then spoke again. "Captain, what about the exchange of technical personnel?"

Picard frowned. A few days ago, Geordi had reported he'd been contacted by Brutus Nothus, the chief engineer of the *Centurion,* who had suggested that the two ships exchange technical personnel to facilitate the work on the satellite network.

"Do you still think such an exchange would be useful?" Picard asked.

"After the work they did here?" Geordi sounded somewhat surprised by the question. "Captain, they've put some security features on this net that are light-years ahead of what we've got. Plus, the phasers on the satellites are all linked together in such a way that the power-utilization curve is the most efficient I've seen on a system this size. I'd love the chance to find out more about how they pulled that one off."

Of course, Picard thought. Security interlocks, highly efficient weapons systems—they would be expert at such things.

"Such exchange of personnel is a fairly common procedure, sir," Worf said, "Regulations stipulate—"

"I know the regulations, Lieutenant," Picard said impatiently. He shook his head. *You're acting unreasonably. This won't do, Jean-Luc! A bit of personal animosity, and you behave in this silly way. Come now!* He could almost hear the voice of Monsieur du Plessis quoting one of those hoary old maxims he so favored: *Envy is more irreconcilable than hatred.*

Picard nodded. "Very well. Mr. La Forge, contact Brutus Nothus and begin bringing some of their people over here to work with your subordinates."

"And what about sending some of our people over there, Captain?"

Picard paused in thought, then said, "Not yet." He closed the channel before Geordi could question his reasons.

Sorry, monsieur, he thought. *That's as far as I feel able to go for now.*

"That's as far as I'm going," Riker said. He flopped down on a large boulder and dropped the pack he was carrying beside him.

Gretna shook her head and studied the valley floor below them.

"We'll be there in a half an hour, Will," she said.

"You said that half an hour ago." Riker wiped the sweat from his brow and took a sip from the canteen hanging on his belt. It was hot, and he was glad to be wearing native clothing—shorts, loose cotton shirt, and moccasins—rather than the standard Starfleet uniform. *Otherwise, I'd have drained my canteen about ten miles back.*

Gretna sat down by his side and pulled a roughly sketched map out of her knapsack. "According to this, the village should be just past that stream." She pointed down the valley at a riverbed perhaps a mile distant. "A lot has changed here over the last few years—that's how I lost my bearings."

Riker knew what she meant. They had passed evidence of the M'dok attacks everywhere on their journey across the countryside—patches of razed forest, the burned-out remnants of a village—yet the land was indescribably beautiful. They were journeying across what was once Tenara's breadbasket, a valley about four hundred miles outside Zhelnogra. Their survey was intended to help the Federation evaluate what the Tenarans needed to rebuild their world and what aid they would require, though from what Riker could see, nature was capable of taking care of most of the M'dok-inflicted scars herself.

"This is a beautiful country—better than any holodeck illusion," Riker said quietly.

"Better than any what?" Gretna asked.

"Never mind," he said, shaking his head. It would take a long time to explain the workings of the holodeck. "All right," he said, climbing to his feet. "A half-hour—but that steak you promised me had better be as good as advertised. Because I'm—"

"—starving," she said, smiling. "When we reach Carda, you'll have the best food and drink the inn can provide—I promise you."

Gretna, he had discovered, had lived in this part of Tenara for a few years, before moving back to the capital where she'd been born. He had discovered many things about her over the last few days—none of which were lessening the powerful attraction he had felt at their first meeting.

"Look." Riker pointed. A thin plume of smoke was visible just past the river below.

"That's Carda," Gretna said. "Come on."

About twenty minutes later they came to a small clearing and a group of five or ten buildings.

The M'dok had obviously been here as well. Carda was a ruin.

"Oh, no," Gretna said.

There were ten people gathered on the front steps of the largest building, talking among themselves. One by one, they fell silent as Gretna and Riker approached.

One man, short and balding, detached himself from the crowd and stepped forward to meet them.

"It's Larten," she said quietly. "He was the leader of the *saavta* here."

As the man drew closer, Riker could see he walked with a slight limp. There was also a scar (fairly recent, from the look of it), running down one side of his neck, and his eyes were hollow and sunken, as if he hadn't slept for days.

"Gretna," he asked calmly, "what do you want here?"

She stopped in her tracks, dumbfounded.

"What do I want here?" she asked. "I came to see you, to help you."

The man stepped back and eyed Riker—and in particular the tricorder he held—with a mixture of suspicion and resentment.

"What's he doing here?" Larten said.

"Larten, what's the matter with you?" Gretna asked, bewilderment showing on her face. "Is this how you treat guests now? Is this how you treat me?"

"We don't want him or his weapons here," he said coldly. "And if you're with him, we don't want you here either!"

"I don't understand. What—"

"Sari is dead because of people like him!" Larten shouted, his face red. "Our homes are gone—and you ask for welcome?"

"He is nothing like the ones who destroyed your village, Larten," Gretna said.

"He has weapons like theirs!" Larten said. "Now, go!"

Behind him, the other men stepped forward, forming a line behind Larten.

"I think we'd better do as he says," Riker said quietly. "Come on."

Speechless, Gretna let him lead her away from the village.

"What's the matter with them?" she asked.

"They're angry and upset, Gretna. I can't really blame them, after what's happened."

"They're acting like children!" she said. "To blame the Federation for what's happened here . . ."

Riker shook his head. "As I recall from my briefings, a certain Gretna Melkinata was also once strongly against a Federation presence on this world."

"But not now."

"I'm glad about that," Riker said. "Otherwise, you might have *deliberately* lost me in the forest."

"Please don't joke about it, Will!" she said. "These are all my friends, and I *did* side with them—before the attacks, before I saw everything the Federation had to offer us." She was silent a moment. When she looked up, her eyes were full of tears. "Before I met you."

Will Riker didn't know what to say to that. But he did know what to do.

Setting down his pack, he took her in his arms and kissed her.

It had been inevitable that Jenny would accept.

Counting herself, there were ten of them lined up in front of the holodeck entrance, with Gaius Aldus leading the line. *Decurion,* she thought suddenly, wondering if it was a reference from some Roman history course she'd had or simply a rank her mind had created.

She was also, she realized suddenly, the only woman. She wondered briefly if the others resented that, if they perceived her as an intrusion into their fraternal structure. Any such resentment, however, was being kept well hidden in Gaius' presence.

Over the last few days Jenny had finally gotten around to using his first name. And now she was accepting his offer to train with the Magna Romans.

Gaius faced them all briefly. "We will be practicing scenario alpha seven-point-three." From their faces Jenny could see that the Magna Romans were all intimately familiar with that scenario, whatever it might be.

He continued. "Your weapons will be waiting for you inside, as usual. We will move in two finger-fives. *Felicitas.*" He turned back to the door and said, "Holodeck entrance, open."

The doors slid aside smoothly, revealing a dense forest. As always, Jenny was amazed at the accuracy and detail of the simulation. She could smell the leaves, and at the edge of her vision, something that might have been a deer flashed by. She stared around her as they moved inside.

"Holodeck entrance, close," Gaius said, and the incongruity disappeared, leaving them apparently in a huge, nearly trackless forest.

The Magna Romans bent down and picked up objects from the ground, nodding their approval. Jenny looked down and realized that by her feet were a gladius, the Roman short sword, and a sheaf of javelins. There were also a small shield and a suit of armor made of tough leather covered with riveted metal scales—this would be quieter than the segmented plate armor she had seen the *Centurion* personnel wearing during the reception.

After a few seconds' study of the gear, she began putting it on; there had been a time when she had worn very similar equipment as a second skin. The sword was shorter and broader than those she was used to, the shape of the shield slightly different. But these were minor differences indeed, and she felt suddenly much more confident as she looked around her, her hand hovering over her sword hilt in a manner which for years had been as natural to her as breathing.

The Magna Romans were moving into orderly but not too rigid formations. Gaius ended up next to her. "You're in my five," he said quietly. "You know the finger-five?"

"As a starship tactic, not on the ground," she answered, equally low. "But I'm sure I can adapt."

He smiled at her, then moved on to check the rest of his troops. After two more minutes he took his place at the head of the formation, giving a subtle signal, and they began moving.

As her eyes adapted to the dim light of the forest, Jenny could see that it was not at all trackless; faint trails, some animal, some human, were apparent everywhere on the forest floor. She had not the faintest idea where they were going, but Gaius Aldus led the way with surefooted confidence, and she kept formation as best she could, summoning all her old skills, stepping carefully to avoid noise.

What are we doing? she wondered as they moved. *Obviously this is some historical military scenario, but when and where is it set? What's our mission?*

At a point where two trails diverged, Gaius gave a

curious signal which Jenny was quite sure was not Starfleet regulation, and the group halted. At another signal, the second finger-five darted off into the woods along one of the trails, while Gaius' group knelt down, moving slowly and carefully into positions of concealment.

"Now what?" Jenny asked him, whispering.

"Wait."

Soon she heard a group coming along the trail, laughing and talking in a language she did not understand. It sounded like Earth's modern German, but she could make out no words.

Before the group came in sight, there was the sound of a quick movement from the direction in which the other group of Magna Romans had gone. The laughter from up the trail changed to shouts and screams.

Then there was the sound of metal striking metal, and finally the unknown group came in sight, falling back in ragged array as the Magna Romans threw javelins at them and, in some cases, closed in for hand-to-hand combat, thrusting with their swords to deadly effect.

There were about twenty of them, tall, strongly built men wearing animal skins and carrying spears or long swords of a material that looked like bronze. Two had apparently been carrying a slain deer; as Jenny watched, they dropped the animal and drew their swords.

Though the Magna Romans were severely outnumbered, they fought in a disciplined group, holding a line and covering each other, while their opponents apparently lacked any such organization. The enemy tried to turn the fight into a series of single combats, but the tactic was failing miserably.

Jenny started to rise, but Gaius grabbed her arm in an almost painful grip. "Wait!" Then he scuttled away on his belly to a different vantage point, watching the fray intently.

The other Magna Romans were herding their opponents, Jenny realized then, driving them toward the positions held by Gaius' five. Gaius waited until they were about five meters from the concealed positions, and then rose and shouted, "Cast!"

Almost as one, the Magna Romans hurled their javelins, taking the tall barbarians completely by surprise. Even as she straightened her powerful arm, casting her last javelin, Jenny flinched a bit from the sight; their opponents might be only holodeck simulations, but the blood was very red and had a startlingly accurate odor, while the screams of the wounded sounded painfully real.

But adrenaline rushed into her system and then there was no time to think at all. The barbarians were undisciplined but brave, and Jenny found herself face-to-face with one, a mightily built man with a shaggy blond beard, who slashed at her wildly with his bronze sword.

She knocked the blow aside easily with her buckler and thrust for his face. He jumped back, and she saw a new respect come into his eyes.

His next attack was cannier, a feint at her belly and a slash for her throat, but that, too, she blocked, feeling the old excitement and exhilaration of hand-to-hand combat, and thrust straight in for his stomach, low and vicious.

His sword was too high to block, and they were too close for him to jump back; she thrust the sword in and up, driving the sharp blade deep into his vitals, and he dropped his sword, sucking in a last breath in a strangled half-gasp as blood gouted from his mouth.

She pulled her sword out of the crumpling body, staring around wildly, but the battle was over. The barbarians lay "dead" on the ground, already shimmering around the edges as the holodeck dissolved their "bodies."

One of the Magna Romans was lying on the ground, very still, and another one was doubled over in agony, his face white as he held on to a realistic-looking spear that had apparently been driven through his abdomen. He was making odd noises, as though he was trying to scream but couldn't make the proper muscles work.

Before Jenny had a chance to react, Gaius said sharply, "Holodeck, open exit. Simulation, end."

The door opened before them, and the forest scene disappeared, along with Jenny's weapons and equipment. Only she and the Magna Romans were left, standing on a bare holodeck—but the injured personnel were still not moving, and the rapidly spreading pools of blood under them were undeniably real.

Gaius rushed to the other side of the corridor, slapping his hand against a computer panel. "Medical to holodeck," he said urgently. "Two critical."

"On our way," said an answering voice, and then all

was silent except for the horribly labored breathing of the man with the abdominal wound.

The medics were there in seconds, quickly but gently lifting the two men onto flotation stretchers and moving them into the turbolift. Jenny collapsed against the wall, breathing hard. "Gaius, those men . . ."

Gaius put a steadying hand on her shoulder. "Marius should be all right. Julius . . ." He shrugged.

She looked at him, swallowing hard against the sourness in the back of her throat, trying to understand. "The safety interlocks aren't supposed to let things like that happen!"

He shook his head. "My captain had the interlocks taken out of the programming. It's entirely possible to die when using our holodeck."

"Now you tell me," she whispered, breaking away from him. Then she was running, sprinting down the corridor toward the transporter. Confused feelings coursed through her. She was appalled by what she had witnessed. Yet, she still felt a tingle of excitement at the memory of fighting side by side with Gaius.

The only thing she was sure of was her desire to get back to the *Enterprise,* where she could sort through her confusion in peace.

Chapter Six

BUT JENNY FOUND no serenity aboard the *Enterprise*.

There was only one thing to do. She made an appointment to see Counselor Deanna Troi.

Deanna listened to Jenny's story, keeping a straight face with some difficulty. When Jenny finished, Deanna said, "Jenny, have you ever been in love before?"

"No, not really. I . . . Before? What do you mean, before?"

"I mean that you're in love this time."

"But, Counselor, how can that be? That doesn't make any sense!"

"Often it doesn't, although in this case I think it does. You and Gaius Aldus have so much in common —background, training, interests. You're a very attractive woman."

"I am?" Jenny said in surprise.

Deanna laughed. "Yes, you are. And Gaius is a very attractive man."

"Oh, he is!" Jenny said enthusiastically. "And he's both an excellent soldier and a serious student of the theater, and he's so . . . so—"

"I'm sure he is," Deanna said dryly. "So you have a great deal in common, as I said. When you and I were part of the group on the *Centurion* for that banquet, I could sense the physical attraction between the two of you."

Jenny blushed. "Yes," she muttered. "I'd never experienced anything quite like it."

"And," Deanna continued, "since then, you've been thrown together often because of the work you're doing. I would be more surprised if nothing had come of it."

Jenny looked at her eagerly. "So you think it's all right, then?"

Deanna laughed. *"Perfectly* all right, Jenny. I don't know why you think you need my permission, but you have it."

Jenny left with a happy glow, but Deanna sat back to think about more practical matters, which Jenny had not raised. What if this romance did progress, and the two decided to marry? Starfleet had a policy of posting married couples to the same ship, but in this case, which ship would it be? Would Gaius Aldus be willing to leave the service of his captain and lifelong friend? On the other hand, would Jenny be happy if she accepted service under Captain Sejanus on a ship full of Magna Romans?

When the communicator in his cabin whistled, Picard was trying once again to take a nap. *Why do I bother?* He forced himself to his feet. "Picard here."

"Lieutenant Worf, Captain. I'd like to speak to you."

"Fine. I'm on my way."

"No, sir," the Klingon said quickly. "I'm not on the bridge. I'd like to come to your quarters if I may."

Klingon personal problems? Life just refuses to get simpler. "Certainly, Mr. Worf. I'll be waiting for you."

But it wasn't exactly a personal problem that Worf wanted to discuss.

When he showed up a few minutes later, he stood in the doorway looking self-effacing and nervous.

"Come in, Mr. Worf," Picard said with a touch of impatience, "and let the poor door close."

"Sir." Worf stepped in quickly. He waited for the door to slide shut behind him, then said abruptly, "I'd like to be assigned to the surface, sir."

Picard was not entirely surprised, but he pretended to be. He gestured to one of the two well-padded armchairs, and when Worf had sat down, Picard said, "Your role aboard the ship is essential, Lieutenant."

The Klingon shook his head. "I don't believe so, sir. I have subordinates who are quite capable of handling my shipboard tasks for extended periods. In this case, I feel I'm needed on Tenara."

"Are you saying, Mr. Worf, that Ensign de Luz is not capable of handling the job we've assigned to her down there? Remember that it was on your recommendation that she was given that job."

"I did not overestimate her ability, Captain," Worf said, his pride in his subordinate quite apparent. "But I think we did underestimate the task itself."

"According to de Luz's reports, the defensive installations are all in place and properly manned. Commander Riker is supervising other teams from the

Enterprise and the *Centurion,* helping the Tenarans improve their agriculture, transportation, education, and communication. In short, Lieutenant, I can't see what precisely you feel you can contribute. I must also tell you that I'm uncertain about how the Tenarans will react to you. They're not exactly a cosmopolitan people with a wide experience of alien cultures and beings."

Worf almost smiled. "You're afraid I'll terrify them, sir?"

Picard did smile. "In fact, yes."

"That's exactly why I want to go down there, Captain. What I can do—what Jenny de Luz and the others don't have the time to do—is teach the Tenarans how to defend themselves against personal attack by M'dok. In other words, the sort of attack that Quillen told you about. Most of the Tenarans are too peaceful to defend themselves under any circumstances, but some of them react differently. Remember the crowd of Tenarans who almost attacked Jenny, Captain. They have the capacity to fight and defend themselves.

"They'll find me frightening, menacing. But if I can train some of them to defend themselves against me, to fight back if I pretend to attack them. Then they can do it against M'dok too. And those Tenarans I train can be dispersed across the planet to teach the methods, in case of another M'dok ground attack."

Picard sighed deeply. *An army of Tenarans trained in personal combat by a Klingon and dispersed across the planet,* he thought. *What are we doing to the nature of Tenaran society?*

Centuries ago on Earth, a soldier had reported to his superior, in all seriousness, "We had to destroy the village in order to save it, sir." That episode had stood since then as symbolic of the folly of which military organizations were capable. Would future generations read about Captain Jean-Luc Picard's destruction of a society's pacifist nature in order to save it? And if so, would Picard be remembered not only for that folly, but also as the man who had corrupted the nature of Starfleet itself by betraying its own peaceful ideals?

Picard looked up at Worf. "Your arguments have force," he said. "But at this time, I cannot advocate—"

"Captain Picard, to the bridge," Data's voice came over the communicator.

"What is it, Lieutenant?"

"We have picked up two M'dok ships approaching Tenara."

"Computer verifies that they are both M'dok attack craft, on a direct atmospheric entry trajectory," Worf said.

"Full energy to screens," Picard snapped. "Red-alert status. Contact *Centurion* and warn them, just in case—"

"They've just contacted us with the same warning, sir," Worf interrupted. "And put up their own shields," he added.

Picard smiled slightly. "Worf, be ready to fire on the M'dok ships as soon as they come into phaser range— but only at low power. I want to warn them away, not damage them."

Worf's face remained impassive as his fingers played over the tactical console. "Yes, sir."

The M'dok ships drew rapidly closer. Picard stood up and stepped forward, as if the few steps he took toward the main viewscreen were bringing him closer to the M'dok.

"Open a hailing channel," he ordered.

"Channel open, sir." It was Data, at the ops console, rather than Worf at tactical, who replied. The android had switched control over subspace communications to his own console, freeing Worf for any coming action.

"This is Jean-Luc Picard, captain of the USS *Enterprise*. You are about to enter an area we have classified as a red zone. I must ask what your intentions are."

Seconds passed with no reply. On the main viewscreen the spidery shapes of the two M'dok ships became clearly visible.

"At the limits of phaser range, sir," Worf said. "And they've raised their shields."

"No change in course?"

"No, sir." This time it was an Andorian named Hjalmar Foch at the conn. "Still headed directly for atmospheric entry. Suggest we fire soon, sir."

"M'dok ships, this is Captain Picard. Your actions are clearly hostile. You must withdraw from the red zone. I am empowered by Starfleet Command to enforce this order with whatever action I deem necessary."

Still there was no reply. Picard said, "M'dok ships, if you do not withdraw immediately, we will be forced to open fire." He turned to Foch and said, "Mr. Foch, at my order, one-second burst at each ship, with all phasers at lowest power."

"Aye, sir," the young Andorian said with an eagerness that disturbed Picard.

Worf said, "M'dok ships continuing their approach, Captain."

"Fire phasers," Picard growled. "Why?" he muttered to himself. "They must know by now that we can destroy them if we have to."

He was oblivious of the whoosh of the turbolift doors, which opened to admit Counselor Deanna Troi to the bridge. She made her way to her usual seat.

On the viewscreen, two brilliant beams of light speared across the blackness of space, obscuring the starfield as the computer controlling the visual display instantly lowered the illumination level to compensate for the bright flash. The beams diverged slightly, vanishing into what was, to the human eye, empty space.

"Two direct hits," Worf said calmly. "No damage to either ship."

Foch said, "Both changing course now, sir." There was a strained silence on the bridge, during which the computer collected sensor readings on the two M'dok ships. Finally Foch said, "Projection is that they're transferring to geosynchronous orbit, sir."

Picard pursed his lips. "Interesting. Raise our own orbit to geosynchronous, Ensign. We'll keep them in line of sight. And, Mr. Data, keep trying to contact them."

"Yes, sir. Captain Sejanus has requested that you speak with him, sir. As soon as you're free, he said."

"I'm ready now, Data."

"Yes, sir."

Sejanus filled the main viewscreen, replacing the two M'dok ships. "Well done, Captain. But why fire your phasers with no intent to damage or destroy the target?"

Picard rose and stood before the main viewscreen, dwarfed by Sejanus' face, the image of which filled the screen. But even though the image made Sejanus seem like a giant towering over the merely human Jean-Luc Picard, the Earthman met those giant eyes and held them in a contest of equals.

Watching, Troi was struck by the way any meeting between the two men, whether face-to-face or by means of electronic imaging, always contained an element of confrontation. *They're too much the same,* she thought. *The same, but different. There's always mutual respect, but also a contest of wills—brothers and rivals.*

"I choose to appeal to their intelligence and good sense," Picard said. *"If they make any move to attack Tenara, the Enterprise will be within phaser range. That will force them to keep up their shields, which will prevent them from either launching a shuttle toward the surface of Tenara or beaming anyone down to the planet."*

"Stalemate," Sejanus said.

Picard nodded. "That's all that's really needed, Captain. The M'dok will realize that it's pointless to stay here in hopes of eluding us and they'll leave, carrying that message back with them."

"Well-thought-out," Sejanus said. *"Te saluto."* I

salute you. "Not how a Roman would approach the problem, but I believe it is a worthwhile strategy."

The giant face faded away, and the *Enterprise* bridge crew saw the seemingly empty starfield once again.

Picard relaxed. Only now did he realize how tense he had been during his conversation with Sejanus. "Magnification," he called out. "Let's keep an eye on those ships."

The viewscreen display rippled, and then both M'dok ships appeared. The blurring of deflector shields surrounded both.

Picard nodded in satisfaction. "They're not taking any chances. Well, that's what we want. Conn, what's our trajectory relative to theirs?"

"Transfer to geosynchronous orbit under way, sir," Foch replied.

"Mr. Worf, constant surveillance of both M'dok ships. I want no surprises."

"Yes, Captain." Worf was hesitant to speak out on the subject troubling him, but he forced himself to do so. "Captain, may I ask a question?"

"Of course, Lieutenant."

"Sir, Captain Sejanus seemed to be advocating a direct attack on the M'dok ships. It would be possible to follow that advice without causing death or injury to the M'dok, but rather just enough damage to frighten them away from Tenara. As it stands, we're tying down the manpower and scientific resources of the *Enterprise* just to keep these two ships under surveillance."

Picard was impatient. "Your *question*, Lieutenant?"

"Why don't we attack them, sir?"

"Because of who *we* are, Lieutenant." Unsatisfactory as that answer might be, for the moment it would have to do. Before Worf could say anything else, Picard turned to Deanna Troi. "Counselor, can I see you in the ready room?"

"Of course, Captain." The Betazoid followed Picard off the bridge. When the door had shut behind them, cutting them off from the sight and hearing of the crew, she said, "Captain, you seem as worried about Captain Sejanus as you are about the M'dok."

Picard bristled. "I asked you in here to obtain your opinion, Counselor," he snapped, "not to have you analyze me!"

Almost immediately, he apologized. "Sorry. You're right, of course."

He went behind his desk and fell into his chair. He gestured toward a chair facing the desk, and Troi sat down. Though she moved far more gracefully than the captain had, her tension and fatigue almost matched his, because at such close quarters, she felt almost overwhelmed by the powerful negative emotions Picard was transmitting.

He said, "I need to be sure that I'm following the best tactics."

Deanna gestured helplessly. "I can't advise you on that, Captain."

"No, no, of course not," he said quickly. "Nor would I want you to try. Someone said a long time ago that if a starship captain has to order his ship to fire on another ship, then he's already failed in his mission. I suppose that's only a generalization, but you know what they say about generalizations."

"No, Captain. What do they say?"

Picard smiled suddenly. "That no generalization is worth a damn, including this one." His expression grew grim once more. "The choice not to fire on an enemy can be as momentous as the choice to fire. Either can lead to war, either can result in the destruction of a civilization. It's not a morally simple question."

"Few moral questions *are* simple," Deanna observed.

Picard grunted. Then he said, "I grew up surrounded by cats."

The remark might have seemed irrelevant to anyone else; but Deanna sensed its significance, and she waited patiently.

"My parents were unusual in that way." He smiled at the memory. "Some of our neighbors thought they were eccentric. Anyway, they loved both cats and dogs, but cats especially. I grew to love the beasts too, despite the way the creatures destroyed my belongings." He looked at Troi sharply. "I don't mean that I'm confusing the M'dok with the pets I remember from childhood."

"I understand that, Captain. Go on, please."

"What always struck me," Picard said, "was the way our cats watched me to see whether or not I was watching them. As long as they knew I was observing them, they behaved themselves. However, as soon as they thought my attention was directed elsewhere, they would head straight for my room and tear things up. That trait, the M'dok share with them: not exactly deviousness, but rather an aptitude for finding the moment when our attention is diverted. So I want the M'dok to know that we're watching them constantly —that our eyes are not directed elsewhere."

"But you worry about leaving Captain Sejanus behind by himself," Troi concluded.

Picard nodded, mildly surprised at his counselor's intuition. "It's absurd I should feel this way! The man's a Starfleet captain with a brilliant record, commanding a Starfleet ship. And yet I find myself reacting as though he were something else entirely."

"As you know, Captain, I cannot read minds," Deanna said carefully. "I can't tell you what Captain Sejanus actually thinks, sir. All I can do is sense feelings, emotions, attitudes—none of which, I'm afraid, can tell you any more than you already know."

Picard nodded wordlessly.

"The line-of-sight view between ships is psychologically important in sensitive security situations," Picard said obliquely. "Every starship captain knows that. With *Enterprise* in geosynchronous orbit and *Centurion* in standard parking orbit, Sejanus will be out of our direct view roughly two-thirds of the time." He said no more, but he radiated unhappiness and worry.

"Sir, something puzzles me," Deanna said. "After their previous attack ended in the destruction of their ship, why have the M'dok tried to attack Tenara again? Surely they can see it's pointless."

"It would be pointless for us," Picard replied. He

sat on the corner of his desk and stared in thought at the wall opposite. On it was a small framed photograph of Mont St. Michel at high tide, bathed in brilliant sunlight. The ancient monastery had been a favorite of the Picard family during Jean-Luc's childhood, a place they had visited frequently, and usually he found the photograph restfully nostalgic. This time, he didn't even see it. Instead, he saw bloody images of M'dok raids on peaceful farming villages.

Picard shook his head as if that could ward off those terrible images. "The M'dok are a different species. Completely different. They do not reason as human beings do. All we can do is observe their behavior and react to it when necessary. To predict their behavior, we can rely only on experience of their past behavior, not upon logic or our familiarity with our own ways of thinking."

All of this was of course elementary to Deanna Troi, but she knew that Picard wasn't really lecturing her. He was thinking out loud, working his way toward some conclusion.

"Certain things are basic to all creatures," he continued. "Hunger is one. This famine in their empire is terribly severe. It may be that the M'dok are mad with hunger. Or they may feel humiliated by their earlier defeat." He paused, then added with trepidation in his voice, "Their defeat at the hands of Captain Sejanus.

"The final possibility is that they may be quite unaware of what happened to that other ship. It may not have sent any kind of message back home before Sejanus destroyed it. In which case," Picard added,

"Sejanus should not have destroyed that ship. I'd much prefer that the M'dok be warned and undertake no further attacks."

"Captain Sejanus' own cultural background may make it impossible for him to see that," Deanna warned.

"Yes. That's what I'm afraid of." Picard grimaced. "If only we knew more about him . . ." He snapped his fingers and pushed a button on his desk.

"Mr. Data," Picard said.

The android's voice came over the intercom. "Yes, sir?"

"I'd like you to research something for me in our historical data base."

"Of course, Captain."

Picard paced slowly about in the wide space between his seat and the operations console. "I'm interested in knowing more about a clan on Magna Roma called the Volcinii *gens*. At least, I assume it's a clan; that's what *'gens'* meant in ancient Latin. I want to know about their past, their present, and their cultural significance."

"I will do my best, sir," Data replied.

"I know you will, Lieutenant." Picard closed the channel and looked up at Deanna. "Is there anything else, Counselor?"

"Well . . . yes, sir. It seems to me that normally, with two ships like ours stationed together this way, there'd be a great deal of fraternization between the two crews. But with the *Enterprise* and the *Centurion*, that has never happened. I was just wondering if that was your decision or Captain Sejanus'. If you don't mind my asking."

Picard grunted. "I do mind, but I've found that you tend to ask anyway."

"Yes, sir. It's my duty."

"And your inclination?"

"Perhaps my nature, sir."

Picard smiled, then laughed. "Fair enough, Counselor. The truth of the matter is that I've not initiated any kind of joint social activities between the crews, and I've managed to avoid approving any requests for such activities that have come my way. I admit readily that my reasons aren't based entirely on reason. I respect Sejanus professionally, but I dislike him personally. Admittedly, this is an irrational basis for command decisions. I must tell you that the *Centurion* hasn't made any overtures to us for social events, either. Perhaps Sejanus feels the same way toward me. Is that the explanation you expected, Counselor?"

"Pretty much," she admitted. "Captain, I would like your permission to initiate such activities with the *Centurion*—on a limited basis."

"What do you suggest?"

"Well, first I'd like to visit the *Centurion*, talk to their ship's counselor, maybe Captain Sejanus as well."

"I can read your mind," Picard suggested with some irony. "You want to visit the *Centurion* and see what Sejanus is really made of."

Deanna smiled. "I wish I *could* see that much. But, yes, I would like to speak to him in person to get more of a sense of his true self. For a number of reasons, sir." She told Picard about her meeting with Jenny.

"I would hate to lose an officer like de Luz," Picard said.

"So do I have your permission to visit the *Centurion?*"

"Very well, Deanna."

As she turned to go, Picard was suddenly seized with the urge to tell her to be careful.

Ridiculous.

During the hours that followed, the *Enterprise* kept a geosynchronous orbit, with the two M'dok ships always within direct line-of-sight sensor view. Under Picard's standing orders, whenever either M'dok ship dropped its shields, the *Enterprise* increased the power to its own shields and approached closer to the M'dok ship in question. Each time, the M'dok responded by quickly raising their shields again. As Picard had intended, the M'dok could not use their phasers or transporters, and their power levels were slowly but steadily decreasing. Sooner or later, Picard hoped, they would give up and leave Tenaran space, headed for home.

Or something else would happen.

"Civis Tenarus sum," the little boy said carefully, frowning at the floor. Then he looked up quickly at Marcus, seated in the teacher's chair at the front of the classroom. They were using the large room that occupied the entire ground floor of the building. The smaller rooms upstairs, intended as classrooms, made

Marcus feel somewhat claustrophobic—and struck him as traps if the locals turned hostile. Down here, with lots of space around him, he felt closer to escape at all times. Moreover, he had commandeered two of the upstairs rooms and, after having locks installed on the doors, had filled them with personal items and textbooks beamed down from the *Centurion*.

When the boy saw that the Roman was smiling at him approvingly, he laughed in relief, and his classmates joined in his slightly nervous laughter.

"Excellent, Claudius!" Marcus said, beaming at the class. "Children, you're really working hard at your lessons. Why, if this were Magna Roma, you'd all be candidates for senatorial scholarships." The boys and girls—all under ten years old—occupying the rows of desks before him had no idea what a senatorial scholarship was, but they could tell that he was complimenting them, and beamed with pride. They were all intrigued by the idea of being Magna Roman students. It was a change of pace from boring, dull, everyday life on Tenara. One of the girls raised her hand.

Marcus nodded at her. "Yes, Julia?" Her name was actually Yoolka, but in the classroom each child used a Roman name assigned by Marcus. The boy he had called Claudius was really named Klamnin.

Yoolka said, "Magister, you promised that today you'd tell us all about the conquest of Africa."

"So I did, Julia. Yes . . . an exciting part of Magna Roman history, full of the heroic deeds of great men. It's also a period of our history that greatly influenced the centralized form of our government. It took less than a hundred years to add that entire continent to the empire, but the roots of the conquest were sown far back in Roman history, so let's begin with the fall of Carthage. Remember what I told you about the Punic Wars? . . . Good." Before he could continue, Marcus became aware that the children's attention had been diverted by something behind him. He jumped to his feet and turned.

A woman in native costume stood in the doorway of the classroom. She was tall, with a strong, intelligent face.

She was also quite beautiful.

Marcus raised his eyebrows questioningly at her.

"Please pardon my intrusion," she said without a trace of apology in her voice. "You're from Starfleet, aren't you?"

"Quite correct. I'm Marcus Julius Volcinius."

"Gretna Melkinata," she said, bowing. She locked eyes with Marcus. "I'm here with some of the *Enterprise* crew."

"Oh?" Marcus said.

"Yes, we're surveying the needs of the local populace throughout this valley." She stared directly at him. "Forgive my bluntness, but what exactly are you doing here?"

"He's teaching us about Rome!" one of the children shouted out.

Marcus gestured expansively. "I was sharing some of Magna Roma's rich history with my new pupils."

"I see. *Your* pupils. And where are their regular teachers?" she asked evenly.

"In the valley, joining their comrades in farming while I broaden these children's horizons. It's part of our cultural-exchange program."

Gretna nodded. "And who has authorized this program?"

Marcus closed the distance between them and spoke quietly. "I understand your concern, but I assure you that I am operating on the highest authority."

"Really?"

Marcus nodded. "Perhaps you would like to return this evening and discuss our plans for the exchange program and the additions to the curriculum. I'd be happy to show you my authorization papers as well, but now I'm afraid that I must return to my students."

"Of course," Gretna answered with a tight smile as she turned to go. "Tonight, then."

She left, and Marcus quickly finished the lessons for the day. After the last of the children was gone, he headed for the building's stairway.

On the upper floor, Marcus stopped in front of one of the heavy wooden doors. A flat male computer voice said, *"Nomen."*

"Marcus Julius Volcinius."

"Confirmatus."

The lock clicked, and Marcus pushed the door open. His ancestors would have thought the whole process wondrous. To Marcus, used to doors that slid aside for him, the need to actually push on the door so that it swung on its primitive hinges was a chore that seemed a worse burden every time he did it.

Once inside, he pushed the door shut, listened for the click of the lock engaging, and then turned to the small communications viewscreen on a wooden table in the center of the room.

Gretna Melkinata's inquiries presented him with no small problem, one that could possibly affect all his plans here . . . and elsewhere.

Chapter Seven

IT WAS BARELY AN HOUR after sunset, and already the entire village was dark, its streets deserted. The only flash of color in the sky came from the stars above— and the flicker of the schoolhouse lights ahead of her.

People went to sleep early on Tenara. Not surprising, since most of them spent the day hard at work and had to be up at the crack of dawn for another day of backbreaking physical labor.

Except for father and me, Gretna Melkinata thought. *Two bureaucrats on a planet full of farmers.*

As a little girl, she remembered staying up to the wee hours watching her father work, reading, writing, preparing legislation and speeches. As she grew older, he had let her help, even occasionally talked through his ideas with her, especially after her mother had died. It was a kind of talk that few people on Tenara were interested in, except for other old men.

So she had been greatly pleased to discover politics was a topic Will Riker knew and enjoyed.

"Part of the job," he'd told Gretna last night, over dinner around a campfire, their unsettling experience at Carda several hours behind them. "After all, we're the first Federation representatives that many worlds meet. And the leaders of those worlds, if they want to join the Federation, want to know how their own governments will be affected by membership."

"You're the only person my age I've met who likes to talk about these things," Gretna said.

"Oh, I can't believe that."

"It's true!" Gretna said. She pulled the vegetables she'd been cooking out of the fire and set them aside to cool. "I can remember going to school, back when the Federation first came here, and trying to talk about these things with the others. They avoided me like I was crazy," she said.

"The *boys* avoided you?" Will asked, a glint in his eye.

She couldn't help but smile. "Well . . . they didn't necessarily want to talk."

"That, I can believe."

Gretna shrugged. "Maybe it was that I just knew so much more about it than any of them, since my father was in charge of the committee to restructure the government."

Will took a hunk of bread out of his carrysack, broke off a piece, and began to chew on it thoughtfully. "I didn't know that."

Gretna nodded. "The whole idea of the *saavtas* was his. He wanted to preserve the independence of the smaller communities and still have a governmental body powerful enough to make decisions for the whole planet."

"That's always the problem," Will said. "How

powerful can you let the central government become before it loses touch with the people and becomes a dictatorship?"

Gretna reached into her knapsack and pulled out a canteen. "Some *jhafre?*"

Will nodded. "Sure."

"How did you settle that on your home planet?" she asked, handing him the canteen.

"Well . . . I can't say that we *did* settle it," Will said. "The whole question became obsolete, in a way, because technology helped us outgrow the need for that kind of government. I, for one, have always agreed with Rousseau—one of our philosophers— who said true democracy and a large central government were irreconcilable goals." He took a swig out of the canteen and made a face. "What is this stuff?"

"Jhafre—ale."

"Ale? You mean it's got alcohol in it? Real alcohol?"

Gretna nodded, slightly confused. "Of course. What else?"

Will shook his head. "Never mind. I'm going to regret this in the morning, but"—he took a long swallow—"at least it's better than that Magna Roman appetizer."

Gretna looked at him questioningly, so he told her about the banquet aboard the *Centurion.*

She thought for a moment before speaking again. "What about the Magna Romans?" she asked. "How did they solve the problem—reconciling a democracy with a large central government?"

Will stared at her. "Did I ever tell you how perceptive you are for a naive Tenaran girl?"

"Yes." She took the canteen back from him. "Now answer the question."

"I'm not sure the Magna Romans," Will said, speaking carefully, "ever solved that problem either —until the Federation solved it for them."

The next day, thinking about his answer, Gretna shuddered. What, exactly, was Marcus Julius teaching the schoolchildren here? And how high up did his authorization go?

Suddenly she wished Will was with her now—he'd get some straight answers out of the Magna Roman. But he'd taken the other agronomists from the *Enterprise* on a survey expedition this morning, and wasn't due to rendezvous with her until early tomorrow.

And besides, what if Will already knew what Marcus was up to? She didn't want to believe that, but for her planet's sake, she couldn't let her personal feelings for him get in the way of facts. *He is part of the Federation, as are the Magna Romans.*

"Gretna."

The voice, coming from beside her, was so unexpected that she almost jumped out of her skin.

She turned, and Marcus Julius Volcinius was standing there, smiling.

"Sorry if I frightened you." He moved around in front of her. "I was just on my way back from the village and thought I saw you standing out here."

Marcus was now dressed in a maroon Starfleet uniform, identical to the one Will had been wearing when she first met him. He was a good half-foot shorter than she, and somehow that made her initial shock easier to overcome.

"I'm not frightened," Gretna said, "I'm angry. I want to know what you're doing with the children in there." She jerked a thumb back toward the schoolhouse.

"Of course," Marcus said smoothly. "I'd be happy to explain—or more precisely, someone else will."

"I warn you, I'm in no mood for games, Marcus Julius."

Marcus shook his head. "This is no game. I need to take you to where the decision to undertake the program was made—and to the people who decided to make it."

Gretna eyed the Magna Roman dubiously. Was he trying to trap her? To get her somewhere out of the way and kill her? No, she decided. He's crafty enough for it, but too many people know where I am.

"All right," she said. "I'll be interested to see who among you thinks he has the power to make this decision."

Marcus smiled. "You are familiar with the transporter?"

She nodded. "I've never actually used one, but—"

"We need it to get where we're going." Marcus touched the insignia on his chest.

Centurion, this is Marcus Julius. Ready to transport."

He lowered his hand and smiled at her. "Relax. This won't hurt a bit."

Gretna stood stock-still for a moment, then felt a strange tingling in her body. She felt faintly sick, and then . . .

They were standing in the Central Council Chamber, back in the Tenaran capital city of Zhelnogra.

She looked around in surprise. "What are we doing here?"

"You've come to see us."

She spun at the sound of the new voice.

Another man in Starfleet uniform was standing there smiling at her.

"You remember Captain Sejanus." Marcus nodded. "And of course . . ."

Another figure stepped out of the shadows.

". . . Captain Picard of the *Enterprise*."

Gretna nodded, too surprised to speak. If Picard knew what was going on, then Will knew. She felt like a fool.

"All right," she said angrily. "Tell me why you three think you have the right to interfere in our affairs—in the education of our children. And make it good," she said, crossing her arms, "so I can tell my father."

"Your father already knows."

Gretna spun, unable to believe her ears.

Melkinat stood there smiling at her. "Daughter," he said, "I am glad to see you."

"Father!" Gretna rushed to him, and threw herself into his arms. "What are you doing here?"

"Captain Sejanus asked me to come, child."

She took a step back, holding him at arm's length. "Then you know what this man is doing, what he's teaching?"

Melkinat nodded. "Marcus' program is the only way to save our planet from the M'dok, daughter. Once the Federation leaves . . ."

Gretna's head was spinning; how could this be real?

"No," she said weakly.

"Once the Federation leaves," Melkinat continued, "we will have to be strong, to be able to defend ourselves."

Over Melkinat's shoulder she could see Marcus smiling at her.

"Why didn't you tell me about this?"

"I'm sorry—I should have. But I feared you would tell the others—Anka and her group—and we would lose this chance to educate our people. And," he said, bowing his head, "I feared you would think less of me for not consulting with you. But I know I'm right."

She shook her head, barely aware that Picard was now speaking.

"It's a program designed to make your people self-sufficient, Gretna. Marcus is an excellent teacher."

Melkinat took his daughter's arms. "Forgive me . . . please."

She twisted free. "I cannot believe this." She turned to Marcus. "I want to get out of here. Now."

"As you wish," the Magna Roman said. He tapped his communicator insignia. *"Centurion."*

"Centurion here, sir."

"Beam the chairman's daughter back to our original coordinates."

"Aye, sir."

Gretna bit her lip and turned back to her father. "I need some time to think."

"Promise me you won't do anything rash, child." He looked at her again. "I love you."

She nodded weakly—and then she was gone.

Marcus laughed. "'I love you,'" he said, mimicking the chairman's voice. "Now, that was a nice touch."

"Thank you," Melkinat said stiffly.

"And you," Marcus said, turning to Picard. "I thank you for the recommendation. 'Marcus is an excellent teacher'—indeed."

Picard stood motionless. "I was happy to be of help."

"You were exceedingly helpful." Marcus nodded. "Simulation end."

The forms of Melkinat and Captain Picard faded and disappeared. The outlines of the council chamber wavered, and suddenly Marcus was standing in the *Centurion*'s holodeck chamber.

Sejanus laid a hand on his shoulder. "Well-played, cousin. Well-played. That should keep the girl quiet until tomorrow, which will be quite long enough."

"Thank you, my lord." Marcus turned and knelt before his captain. Sejanus was dressed in a purple robe and wore a toga of Magna Roman design beneath. "I am, as always, at your service."

When Deanna materialized on the *Centurion*'s transporter platform the next morning, she was met, as she had expected to be, by Julia Sicania, the *Centurion*'s counselor. What she had not expected was that Captain Sejanus would be there too.

It was Julia whom Deanna had contacted to request a tour of the ship. The Magna Roman counselor was a woman of about forty, but with the signs of premature aging on her face. She had responded to Deanna's request bluntly: "Why? What business do you have here?"

Outwardly calm, though inwardly furious at this treatment, Deanna had smiled and said, "I wish to compare the social structures aboard our two ships. The societies the crews come from are very different, and I think it would be educational for me, professionally speaking, to see how you've resolved your problems."

Julia had grunted something and said she would have to see if such a visit could be arranged. However, only minutes later she had called back and extended a very polite invitation to Deanna to beam over at her convenience. There had been something cowed in Julia's manner during that second conversation.

Now, as soon as Deanna materialized, she felt herself swimming in the powerful emotions filling the room, and the explanation for the difference between her two conversations with Julia Sicania became clear.

The hatred and resentment the *Centurion*'s counselor felt toward her captain blazed from her; Julia made no attempt to suppress it. From Sejanus, Deanna caught first his contempt for and then his annoyance with his counselor. Deanna realized immediately that Julia had not wanted to be bothered with her but had been overruled by Sejanus. Then came a secondary impression from the two Magna Romans: a powerful current of something in their past, some close and passionate relationship that was now over.

The Magna Romans were both unfamiliar with Betazoids, or perhaps did not know that Deanna was half Betazoid. She could detect no wariness in either of them concerning her and no suspicion that she could sense their feelings. They put on appropriate social faces, assuming that they could fool her as easily as they would a human. Julia stepped forward and said brightly, "My dear Commander Troi! We're simply delighted to have you aboard."

Deanna, seeing the true feelings behind that facade, smiled ironically and said, "Counselor. I've been looking forward to meeting you too." She turned to Sejanus. "Captain. How nice to see you again."

She was immediately embarrassed by the wash of primitive emotions coming from him.

Sejanus thought it more than merely nice to see Troi again. "Welcome aboard, Counselor. The first time you were here, we had no chance to talk. I hope we can remedy that."

Deanna raised her eyebrows. "Perhaps after Counselor Sicania shows me the ship, Captain."

Sejanus smiled charmingly. "As it happens, I find myself with a bit of free time on my hands, and thought that I would personally conduct your tour. If you have no objections?"

"On the contrary," Deanna said. "That would be lovely."

"Excellent. We'll begin right away." He let Deanna precede him through the door. In the hallway outside, Sejanus said, "I thought we'd begin with our engineering deck."

Deanna laughed. "Captain Sejanus, I've seen all I ever want to of matter-antimatter chambers."

"Of course," he replied. "I forget that you come from a Galaxy-class vessel beside which even the splendors of this ship must pale."

"Perhaps your schools," Deanna suggested. "I'm very interested in finding out more about what makes your society such an energetic, vital one."

"This way, then." Sejanus led her down a long corridor and past one turbolift.

She stopped at one door behind which she heard crying.

"What's this?" she asked.

"Sick bay," Sejanus replied.

"May I?" Deanna stepped through the door before he could reply.

Sick bay on the *Centurion* consisted of a single room with half a dozen narrow diagnostic beds crammed into it. Against one wall stood a small desk. One crew member was on duty when they arrived, a short, slender, dark-skinned, curly haired young man, extremely nervous in the presence of his captain, who leapt to his feet when Sejanus appeared and snapped the chest-slapping, extended-hand Roman salute.

Sejanus responded with a nod. "At ease, Doctor. Counselor, this is Dr. Marius Tertius Secondus, second-in-command of our medical section. Marius, this is Lieutenant Commander Deanna Troi, from the *Enterprise.*"

Deanna greeted the doctor, then looked around in surprise. "Is this all of your sick bay, Doctor?"

"Why, yes, Commander. It's usually adequate."

"Usually!" She didn't try to hide her shock. "This

ship has almost half the complement of the *Enterprise,* and yet we have three or four times as much room and equipment in our sick bay!"

Marius was obviously floundering for a reply. Sejanus took over. "We emphasize other kinds of care instead. All of our personnel are quite competent at first aid for minor injuries, and our injured convalesce in their own quarters."

Deanna managed to keep her voice even this time. "What about an illness of some kind affecting large numbers of people? Some sort of plague, for example."

Sejanus smiled. "On my ship, crew members are encouraged not to get ill." He meant the remark to be flippant, but behind the words she sensed his utter boredom with the subject.

Deanna wondered what Starfleet regulations were concerning the minimum size and complement for a starship's sick bay, and if Sejanus was violating those regulations.

"Now, let me show you that school," Sejanus said, taking her by the arm.

As they walked toward a turbolift entrance, Sejanus said, "You'll find some differences between our vessels here, as well. Captain Picard has more specialists of different types among his civilian complement— linguists, agronomists, sociologists, historians, and so on—than I have, and I understand that most of them serve double duty as part-time teachers. Since we have few such experts on this ship, our curriculum is narrower."

When he said the name Picard, Troi sensed a flash

of anger from him, though not a trace of it showed in his voice or on his face. *Jean-Luc will be happy to know his affections are returned,* she thought wryly.

When they reached the area set aside for a school, Deanna found out just how different the curriculum was from that aboard the *Enterprise.*

She saw children of all ages being drilled in Latin and English—and demonstrating, from an early age, impressive proficiency in both. She saw history classes, which concentrated on the history of Magna Roma, with special emphasis on the prerepublican empire. She noted that they covered Federation history quickly and in little depth. Engineering—technology of all sorts—was drilled into the students, but basic science seemed to be given short shrift.

Then they moved on to observe physical-education classes. The training here was rigorous and unforgiving. Troi winced as she saw even small children suffer painful falls or blows from classmates—and then continue as if nothing had happened, stoically enduring their pain. On Sejanus' face she caught a look of pride.

From puberty up, physical education became indistinguishable from military training. And Starfleet regulations would have nothing to say about any of this, she realized: presumably the government of Magna Roma told Sejanus how to run the civilian community aboard his ship. How many of the details did that government know, though?

As they left the school area, Sejanus remarked, "Now you can see why we don't really have human engineering problems on this ship. Magna Roman tradition—discipline. Those are the answers. To my mind, the school is the most important place on the ship. Children are the future of the Roman nation, of course. I take great pride in their achievements—almost as much as I do in the achievements of my crew."

Of course, Deanna thought. *And do all your crew have to undergo the kind of training these children do?*

Would Jenny de Luz have to?

She and Sejanus made small talk at one another all the way back to the transporter room.

"I've enjoyed your company tremendously, Counselor," he said. "I hope to see more of you soon." He took her hand and kissed it.

There was no doubt at all in Deanna's mind about what Sejanus meant by that. She nodded, and stepped up onto the transporter platform. "And I hope to find out more about you, Captain—soon."

Sejanus looked slightly disturbed as she dematerialized.

Deanna went directly to the ready room, where Captain Picard was waiting for her, hands clasped behind his back as he paced in front of the great window that dominated the room.

"Your impressions, Counselor."

"As we knew, Captain, the *Centurion* is a very different ship, run quite differently from this one. It is much more . . . military, and there is a great deal of emphasis on maintaining Magna Roman values."

Picard chose his words carefully. "An . . . unacceptable emphasis?"

Deanna sighed heavily. "No, sir. Everything was in

order . . . and yet I must tell you that I now feel your suspicions of Sejanus are justified. He is not what he seems, sir."

Picard leaned against the glass, resting his head on a clenched fist. "Then what is he?"

Deanna shifted uncomfortably, sensing her captain's frustration. "That, I cannot be sure of, sir—not without another visit."

The door chime sounded.

Picard turned. "Come."

Data was standing in the doorway.

"I have the information you requested on the Volcinii gens, Captain," the android said.

Picard fell into his desk chair, suddenly overwhelmed by a wave of fatigue. "Go ahead, please, Mr. Data. Counselor, stay," he told Deanna. "You'll be interested in this too."

The android cleared his throat—purely a theatrical gesture, a deliberate imitation of human speech patterns, Picard was convinced—and said, "You were quite correct, Captain, about the word *'gens.'* As in ancient times, it still refers to a clan, a group of families, the heads of each of which claim descent from a common ancestor—in this case, presumably someone named Volcinius, who may or may not have been a real historical figure. The parallels with the clan structures in ancient times on other Federation worlds are intriguing," he continued, warming to his subject. Then he caught sight of Picard's expression and said, "However, this is not the proper time or place to pursue them.

"The Volcinii *gens* was a patrician family during

imperial times, and quite powerful. Moreover, they were steadily building their wealth and political influence. Had the old empire continued, they might well have managed to put one of their own members on the throne in time."

"They must have been unhappy to see the empire fall, then," Deanna remarked.

"Actually, they had prepared themselves quite well for that possibility. Although they could hardly have foreseen the events which precipitated the fall of the empire and the establishment of the present republic, they had long maintained good contacts with all parties, including the democratic forces which took over when Proconsul Claudius Marcus and his puppet, the last emperor, were overthrown. Early in the revolution, the Volcinians threw in their lot with the revolutionary army."

As Picard already knew, the fall of the empire was the direct result of the visit to Magna Roma—or planet 892-IV—of an earlier USS *Enterprise*. The proof that there were other worlds where sanity ruled, rather than brutality, emboldened the democratic revolutionaries and, five years later, led to the collapse of the imperial government. Soon afterward, the newly established Republic of Magna Roma joined the Federation.

"How long has it been since the revolution on Magna Roma, Data?" Picard asked.

"About seventy years, sir."

"And during that time, surely the Volcinians haven't been able to retain the power and influence they had in the old times—even with their supposed sympathy for democracy."

"I believe the new republican government shared your skepticism about the Volcinians' sincerity, sir. The *gens* was steadily excluded from governmental positions, and the electorate did not treat Volcinians kindly when they ran for office. However, time is a great healer of painful memories, and the people of Magna Roma inevitably forgot the important role the Volcinians had played in the oppressive government of imperial times."

Picard nodded. "How closely is Captain Sejanus connected to the *gens* at this point in time?"

"I do not know, sir."

"Speculate, then."

"Very well," Data said. "The presence of Marcus Julius Volcinius aboard the *Centurion*, even in an advisory role, suggests that the *gens* is very much aware of every move Sejanus makes."

"And possibly guiding his actions?"

"No, sir," Data said. "We are too far away from Magna Roma for such communication to be efficient."

Deanna nodded. "But certainly, as Sejanus' reputation grows—"

"So does that of his family." Picard stood and began pacing. "What if he plans to put the Volcinii *gens* back in power?"

"They will all have to be elected by the Magna Romans, Captain," Deanna pointed out. "Just being related to Sejanus won't get them into office."

"Perhaps Sejanus' goal is not political office for the *gens,* sir," Data said, "but for himself."

Picard stopped pacing. Even in democratic nations, successful generals had come home from war to public acclaim and electoral success. Was that the path Captain Lucius Aelius Sejanus intended to follow?

He turned to the window again. Somewhere out there were the two M'dok ships—and Captain Sejanus and the *Centurion.*

What, indeed, were any of them planning?

"What do you want me to do, Jenny?" Gaius asked, a slight annoyance creeping into his voice. "I have neither the authority nor the desire to countermand the captain's override of the safety interlock."

"But, Gaius, it's not right for people to die! It's only an exercise!"

Gaius shook his head. "It's not that simple, Jenny. Soldiers don't take the simulated exercises seriously enough if they know they're not in any real danger. They're too casual about the whole thing. Then, when they find themselves in a real situation—"

"I know that argument," Jenny interrupted. "I've heard it from you before. I don't buy it."

Gaius sighed. "Well, we'd better agree to disagree, then. Since you feel so strongly about it, why don't you stay out here this time?"

Jenny folded her arms and glared at him angrily. "Maybe I will."

"Good." Gaius turned toward the holodeck entrance, but took only two steps before he spun back to face her. "In fact, perhaps you shouldn't come over here for these exercises anymore, given your opinion of how we do things."

"I should just wait out here while you go in and get yourself killed by a computer-generated barbarian, is that it?"

"I haven't been killed yet!" Gaius said, practically yelling. "Look—"

Jenny suddenly put a hand over his mouth. "We're being watched."

Gaius stopped talking and turned to his left.

Half a dozen Magna Roman soldiers waiting to enter the holodeck were watching with great interest.

"What are you looking at?" Gaius snapped. "Get in there"—he indicated the holodeck—"and get that camp set up!"

The soldiers scrambled to obey.

Gaius took Jenny's arm and led her a short distance down the corridor. "I worry about you during the exercises as well," he said in a low voice.

"Do you?" Jenny's anger evaporated at his words.

"Of course I do . . . but I still won't change the way things are. These are exercises to prepare for life-and-death situations. A single mistake, and—"

"All right." Jenny admitted defeat for the moment. "Let's go in there together and watch each other's backs."

What followed in the holodeck was similar to Jenny's first experience of the *Centurion*'s training simulations. The enemy was the same—German tribesmen—and the ambush tactic was also the same. But there were also differences, the most important of which was that no real humans died. Only simulations were killed, and none of those deaths happened close enough to Jenny to seem real. The other major differences were the sizes of the opposing forces and the setting.

This time, the fighting was the Battle of Britannia, which historically marked the turning point in the long Roman war against the Germans. The German tribes united for long enough to send a combined army by sea. They had purchased transport from their northern neighbors, the Norse, to attack the great Roman city of Londinium, which they thought was undefended. It was to be the battle to destroy Roman power and prestige in the West. Instead, it was a trap, carefully laid by Roman army strategists.

The German army landed in southern Britannia and advanced rapidly toward Londinium. It wasted little time on pillaging as it went, for the greater prize awaited. However, the seemingly empty meadows were virtually saturated with carefully hidden Roman legions. When the trap was sprung, the surprise was complete, and it was German power that was broken, not Roman.

The purpose of this holodeck exercise was to train officers for battlefield command, rather than to expose them to hand-to-hand combat. Gaius was in supreme command of the legions waiting in hiding, and those who had entered the holodeck with him were in various subsidiary command positions with those legions or on his staff. Gaius had to use runners and youths on fast horses to keep track of the advancing Germans and to transmit his orders to his legions; none of the communication technologies taken for granted by Starfleet personnel were available to him. Thus it was quite possible for the officer being subjected to this exercise to mishandle his command badly enough so that the Germans won this replay of the Battle of Britannia.

"What would happen then?" Jenny asked. They were in the command post in the outskirts of Londinium. Behind them lay the silent city. Before them were the rolling plains, silver in the moonlight, across which the Germans were advancing toward them. The Germans were still out of sight of their naked eyes—which was all they had in this simulation—as were the hiding legions. At least they could talk in normal voices instead of whispering.

"I suppose the Germans would overrun us and kill us all," Gaius replied.

Jenny could hear the tension in his voice. She put her hand gently on his forearm. The muscles were knotted, quivering slightly. "Not if you told the computer to end the simulation quickly enough."

Gaius smiled tightly. "With the score the machine would give me for losing the Battle of Britannia, I'm not sure I'd want to survive."

"Couldn't you just follow exactly the same tactics the historical general did?"

Gaius shook his head. "These Germans don't follow the same tactics the historical ones did. Wouldn't be much of an exercise that way, would it?"

Jenny took her hand away. She was sure he hadn't felt it anyway.

"There!" cried one of the officers.

Far away, invisible but for the flashes of light

reflecting from their spears and axes, the Germans came. As they moved, Jenny's keen eyes picked out more of them; they were spread in a long line, and the dust of their movement was clear long before individuals came into view.

The Germans had been canny enough to send scouts north to the mouth of the Tamesis River, which divided Londinium in two, and then toward the city; but the Romans had anticipated that, and the scouts had found nothing. Now this scouting party was moving to rejoin the principal group, and the main battle party was moving toward the city.

Concealed behind the rudimentary wall surrounding Londinium, Gaius flicked his eyes over the approaching Germans. To move too soon would be a disaster, he knew; waiting too long would have less dangerous repercussions. This truth ran contrary to every axiom of Roman military thinking he had been trained in, but it was accurate nonetheless.

Jenny de Luz gasped as the Germans came close enough to make out individual forms. There were thousands of them—surely the only time the barbarians had put aside their tribal differences long enough to form such a huge army—each one a tall, proud warrior with blond or red hair and beard. Each held his spear, sword, or ax confidently in a muscular hand.

Then Jenny saw that they moved in a ragged, disorganized mob, with no structure or order; each warrior moved faster than necessary, each wanting to be the first into the city. Here and there some men rode on horses—tribal chieftains, she assumed—but they made no attempt to bring the formations into order. Instead, they whipped their mounts past their men when they could, so that as the Germans drew closer, the chieftains were at the forefront.

Jenny saw, too, that the Germans were plunging in blindly, paying no attention to the surrounding terrain. As they approached, the line squeezed together, bunching in between the river on one side and a long, low hill on the other. It was a trap that anyone with even the most elementary training in the techniques of land warfare should have been able to spot.

From near-motionlessness Gaius changed to a blur of blinding speed. In his left hand he held a riding whip, which he cracked twice; this was the signal for three young, slender men, nearly unarmored and mounted on the fastest horses, to ride to his subsidiary commanders. They were off instantly, clinging tightly to the horses to keep their saddles as they raced to their destinations.

"Marius!" he snapped to one of the officers standing nearby. "Tell your men to form up near the river. Hurry!"

The man he had spoken to ran to do his bidding.

The German chieftains, mounted on great shaggy horses, waving swords and crying out with wild war whoops, were almost on them. Antonius Appius, a taciturn officer with the quiet deadliness of a snake, made a brief motion with his hand, and ten men stepped forward, each holding a pilum, and cast the heavy spears. The throws all found their marks, and no more than ten meters away, ten men screamed and died. The spear experts picked up another ten pila from the ground and waited.

The remaining chieftains reined in their panicky mounts, realizing that something was going desperately wrong. Then a great shout arose as the Romans marched from the far side of the hill to push the Germans into the river.

The Germans were fierce fighters, as evidenced by the shouts and screams and the noise of metal on metal, which was, even from this distance, nearly deafening. But on level ground, the Romans were and always had been unmatched. The three unwavering lines of Roman infantry pushed steadily onward; when they reached the river, the Germans' advantage of size and weight disappeared, and they were cut down without mercy as they slipped and floundered in the mud.

Those few who managed to turn back the way they had come, trying to escape to the east, were suddenly charged by several hundred Roman cavalrymen, who ran them through with long lances or simply trampled them. Beyond the battle site Jenny saw the water of the river glint red.

A greater problem was the significant number of Germans who had managed to break free of the main Roman line on the west side, facing Londinium. Here, Jenny realized, could be the city's greatest threat, and certainly the greatest danger to their personal safety.

The surviving chieftains, who had been retreating from Antonius Appius' grim spearmen, were heartened by the appearance of their men behind them, and swept forward. Then Marcus Claudius' cohort, three hundred heavy infantry supported on the wings by javelineers and by mounted lancers, executed a perfect left-wheel movement from the river.

The javelin-throwers moved out along the banks, hurling into the thick of the approaching German mob, while the cavalrymen ranged along their flank, herding them toward the infantry.

With a roar, the Germans closed on the infantry. The first line wavered and fell back, but the second line moved quickly to fill the gaps, while the third threw their heavy pila to deadly effect. Within minutes the Germans were all dead or routed, running back toward the east, only to be met by the main body of the Roman troops, who cut them down quickly.

The three mounted messengers came galloping toward Gaius Aldus; they slowed, then dismounted and saluted him.

"All commanders are well," one reported.

"Good," Gaius replied. "Simulation end."

The simulation vanished instantly. Londinium, the spreading plains, the vast numbers of legionaries and German tribesmen all disappeared, leaving a small group of Magna Romans and Jenny de Luz standing scattered about on the naked holodeck.

The lines of worry and tension slowly left Jenny's face. She took a deep lungful of air and blew it out again. *There,* she thought. *The empire is safe again.*

She caught Gaius' eye and smiled.

And so am I.

Chapter Eight

THE WHISTLE OF THE COMMUNICATOR awoke Picard. Data's voice filled the room. "One of the M'dok ships is breaking orbit, sir. You asked to be called if any—"

"On my way," Picard snapped, rolling from the bed.

When he reached the bridge, Wesley Crusher was at conn, and Data in the captain's chair. As Picard headed down the ramp, Data moved quickly to the ops console, taking over from the crewman manning it.

"Status?" Picard asked, seating himself.

"One of the M'dok ships has left, sir," Wesley said. "Looks like it's headed for home."

"And the other ship, Ensign?" Picard prompted. He watched the fuzzy image of the single M'dok ship on the main viewscreen.

"Still in orbit, sir."

"The *Centurion?*"

"Out of our line-of-sight now, sir. She'll be visible again in about half an hour."

Over the next few hours the M'dok would lower their shields at irregular intervals to test the intentions and resolve of the *Enterprise* crew. Instantly Picard would raise shields and move in closer. His meaning was unmistakable: no shuttles, no transporters. The M'dok would raise their shields again just as quickly, and Picard would once again order the *Enterprise* back to its station and its shields lowered to minimum.

The M'dok could have turned on the *Enterprise* and attacked it. Given the nature of M'dok society, Picard was surprised that they did not do so. But such an attack would have been suicide, and perhaps even the M'dok were not given to throwing away their lives to no purpose.

Throughout those boring, potentially deadly hours, Picard sat in the captain's chair, elbow on knee, chin on fist, eyes fixed on the main viewscreen, where the M'dok ship floated. *What was the M'dok's purpose? What were they doing? And where was Sejanus?* The *Centurion* had failed to appear at the expected time, giving Picard cause for concern.

The captain straightened from his brooding position, stood and stretched, his spine cracking audibly in the hush that pervaded the bridge. "Let's give it another try," he announced. "Mr. Worf, hailing frequencies—"

"Captain!" Wesley interrupted. "The *Centurion!*"

"Where are they, Mr. Crusher? Exact position and trajectory."

"Extreme sensor range, coming in from a highly elliptical transfer orbit intersecting ours and the M'dok's."

"Damn him!" Picard said, slamming his fist down

on his own knee and rising from his chair. "The M'dok will see that as an attack. Worf, hailing frequencies open. *Centurion,* this is Picard. Captain Sejanus, break off your approach, do you hear me? Break off your approach!"

Worf cut in. "The M'dok have increased their shields to full power."

Picard shook his head. Damn Sejanus! "Full power to ours, Mr. Worf."

"Centurion shields are up, sir," Data said.

"M'dok firing, sir! On *Centurion!"*

Picard rapped out, "Hold your fire, Mr. Worf."

Wesley said, *"Centurion* on intersection trajectory, sir. Attack mode!"

And then the *Enterprise* crew could do nothing but watch as the *Centurion* approached the M'dok ship at high speed.

The Magna Roman ship fired its phasers at full power. The M'dok ship took the full brunt of the shot, its defensive shields radiating energy in a brilliant rainbow display. Then the *Centurion* hit it with photon torpedoes, and the M'dok shields began to fluoresce dangerously.

"They can't take that much longer," Wesley muttered—a mutter that everyone on the bridge could hear. "Why don't they respond?"

Picard knew why not: the *Enterprise.* He could sense the M'dok captain's indecision. If he fired on the *Centurion,* would the other Starfleet ship join the battle? Then his ship would be doomed for sure. The only sensible move was to retreat.

Which he did.

The M'dok ship's shields faded momentarily, and the ship began to move away from the two Starfleet vessels, picking up speed rapidly.

The *Centurion* followed.

"Should we break orbit and follow, sir? In case Captain Sejanus needs our help?" Wesley asked.

"No," Picard said firmly. "Absolutely not. Our assignment and our responsibility is to protect Tenara. Just keep both ships on the main viewscreen." *If Sejanus does get himself into trouble, I'll have no choice but to go to his aid.*

The main viewscreen showed the running battle. The *Centurion* was right behind the M'dok ship, pouring huge amounts of energy into it in the form of phaser bolts and photon torpedoes.

"The M'dok are only moving at about one-tenth warp, sir," Worf said. "That first barrage from the *Centurion* must have crippled them."

There was something unspoken in what Worf said: approval of Sejanus' tactics. Picard understood the Klingon to be saying that if one were forced to fight, then that was the way to do it. Picard hoped that Worf had not failed to see how unnecessary it had been for Sejanus to fight at all—that it had been the appearance of the *Centurion* on the scene, coming in unexpectedly from deep space, that had precipitated the battle.

"Turning and fighting, at last," Worf said with undisguised satisfaction. "The only choice left to them at this point."

"A channel to the *Centurion*, Mr. Worf," Picard said.

"Channel open, sir."

"Captain Sejanus," Picard said, "I urge you to break off this engagement now, before there are casualties."

Sejanus' face filled the screen. "We—"

A loud burst from the M'dok ship indicated that the fight was truly joined—and suddenly the uneven battle no longer seemed so uneven.

The M'dok counterattack was vicious and unrestrained. The percentage of energy they were diverting from their deflector shields to their phasers was almost total—and the Magna Romans found themselves under such heavy bombardment that they were in no position to take advantage of that lowering of the M'dok shield energy.

"*Centurion* taking some damage," Worf said. "Their shields will be in danger soon, at this rate."

At some level, Picard had known it would come to this—to his being drawn into a battle by Sejanus, into being forced to take lives and to endanger his ship. "All right! We'll go to help them. Mr. Crusher, lay in course and initiate. Mr. Worf, full power to shields. And then full phaser power as soon as range permits."

But even as the *Enterprise* was on its way, the *Centurion* suddenly accelerated directly toward the M'dok ship, full in the face of its continuous phaser barrage.

Still sluggish, and no doubt astonished, the M'dok were unable to maneuver out of the way. The two ships collided at an immensely high closing velocity.

More precisely, their shields collided. Both sets of shields flared as they radiated the kinetic energy that had just been dumped into them. The ships bounced away from each other like rubber balls.

But it had been a glancing blow, and it had been under Sejanus' control. So while the *Centurion* wobbled drunkenly for a moment and then came back under control, its shields low but still intact, the M'dok ship spun away, rotating wildly, and in one area its shields went far too low for safety. As soon as that area rotated back into view, photon torpedoes flashed out from beneath the *Centurion*'s saucer and into the area of weakened M'dok deflector shields.

The M'dok ship exploded soundlessly. The marvelous construction of metal and energy and design, of science and technology, of hardware and software, erupted in a minuscule fragment of a second into a boiling, expanding cloud, glowing in every color, a mad orgy of self-consuming energies.

The terrible image faded, and space was empty once again.

"Captain Sejanus hailing you again."

"On-screen."

Sejanus' face was a mask of confusion. "Picard, why didn't you come to our defense?"

For a moment Picard was too stunned to respond. Then he gathered his wits. "You deliberately forced this encounter, Captain. I do not condone the needless slaughter of an opponent!"

"Needless slaughter!" Sejanus looked surprised. "We are talking about the animals who butchered an entire village—or perhaps you've forgotten that story, Captain!"

"Perhaps you've forgotten what we're doing here," Picard said. "It was the appearance of your ship, and the way you chose to come on the scene, that made the M'dok fight. You forced it."

"If you recall," Sejanus said icily, "we were fired upon first."

"Semantics, Captain," Picard replied. "And what about your own ship and crew? How dare you risk their lives unnecessarily? That engagement should never have happened! The M'dok were fleeing!" His voice had risen in volume. Picard realized he was close to losing control, to shouting out his anger.

"They came to this planet to attack," Sejanus said firmly.

Picard shook his head. "I've been trying to avoid putting you in this position, but you've made it necessary. In addition to the orders Admiral Delapore sent both of us, he also included coded orders specifically to me, giving me the authority to place myself in supreme command of both our ships and the entire Tenaran operation. I didn't want to invoke that order, but your behavior makes it unavoidable, and I am now doing so."

"Why, that's nonsense!" Sejanus blustered. "Why should I believe that?"

Picard straightened again and lowered his voice to its normal level. "I'll have a copy of my orders transmitted to your ship immediately, and of course you can contact Starfleet Command for verification, if you like."

"I'll do that," Sejanus said. "Rest assured, I will most certainly do that."

Sejanus' image disappeared.

"That fool," Picard muttered softly, taking his seat again. *Is he deliberately* trying *to start a war?*

"Picking up an interesting anomaly on the planet's surface, sir," Data said, breaking in on Picard's train of thought.

"What kind of anomaly?"

"We just caught it on our last pass, sir. An unnatural concentration of metallic elements. Coming over the area again now."

"On viewscreen, please."

At first, it seemed to be merely an elongated clearing in the Tenaran forest, with something glittering at one end of it. "Magnification," Picard called out.

The picture ballooned outward, and Picard could see that the clearing was not a natural one—that trees had been shattered and thrown violently aside, that the ground had been plowed up—and that the glittering object was actually many objects, the remnants of a ship.

"M'dok," he said. "But how did they get past us?" He opened a channel to engineering. "Mr. La Forge, what happened to the satellite net?"

Geordi's voice came back clear and strong. "Nothing, sir. It's working just fine."

"An inept landing," Worf said, nodding toward the picture on the viewscreen. "Perhaps it killed them."

Picard shook his head. "Didn't you know that cats have nine lives, Mr. Worf?"

"Sir?"

"Never mind. We'll make no assumptions. Mr. Data, scan the wreckage, please."

"Aye, sir." After a brief pause the android said, "No organic traces in the wreckage, sir."

Picard grunted. "Then they're somewhere in the forest."

He had no need to say any more than that. The forest stretched for thousands of square kilometers below them, impenetrable from above even with their sophisticated instruments. The M'dok could be hiding anywhere in it, and the *Enterprise* would have no way of finding them. Everyone near that crash site was in extreme jeopardy.

Picard rose to his feet. "Mr. Worf, please find Commander Riker for me on the planet's surface. And contact the *Centurion* and have them warn their personnel to be on the lookout for the M'dok. I'll be in the ready room."

"Aye, Captain."

"And, Mr. Data?"

"Yes, sir." The android turned in his chair to look at Picard.

"Find out how they got past us, and make sure it doesn't happen again!"

It took close to half an hour for Worf to locate the *Enterprise*'s first officer. Finally Picard was speaking to Commander Riker's image on the small screen on the ready room's desk.

Picard filled him in on the arrival of the M'dok ships, and the destruction of one of them by the *Centurion.* "Now we've just detected signs of a crash landing on Tenara by another M'dok ship. We can detect no signs of bodies inside the wreckage, so we must assume that the M'dok survived the crash and are now at large on the surface—probably within the forest somewhere outside Zhelnogra, where they are hidden from our sensors. I'm transmitting the coordinates of the crash to you now."

Riker's expression grew tense. "That's very bad news, Captain. Has there been no response from the M'dok Empire to our offers to help them fight the plague?"

"None yet, I'm afraid." He shook his head. "Number One, this may mean war yet."

"I sincerely hope not, sir—especially if Tenara ends up being the battleground." Riker paused. "How did this ship sneak by the satellite net?"

"Commander Data thinks that the two ships we saw were sent to record as many hours as possible of the satellites' sensor broadcasts, so that they could later analyze them and learn to duplicate them. The ship that crashed used that knowledge to dupe the satellites."

"Could they have staged the battle to allow that second ship to sneak by?"

"Absolutely not," Picard said firmly. "Captain Sejanus deliberately provoked that incident."

Riker shook his head. "I still have trouble believing that of a man like Sejanus, sir."

"I have the feeling none of us knows him as well as we thought, Number One." Picard changed the subject. "How's your survey coming?"

"Fine, sir. I'll be sending back preliminary reports tomorrow, but it seems that all the Tenarans will need from us are basic supplies and perhaps a few pieces of heavy machinery to rebuild." He hesitated a moment.

"Are we having problems with the government, sir? With Melkinat?"

Picard shook his head. "I'm afraid I don't understand."

"Well . . ." Riker looked uncomfortable. "I'm afraid his daughter seems to have turned against us—me—over the last day or so. Very strange."

"Nothing you've done, I trust?"

"No sir," Riker said emphatically. "She was supposed to complete the survey with us and then return to Zhelnogra, but now she's gone off on her own. I'm at a loss to explain it."

"Well, contact me again when you rendezvous with her in Zhelnogra. Perhaps one of us will know the reason for her change of attitude then." He exchanged a brief smile with his first officer. "Picard out."

The small screen went dark.

"Mr. Worf?"

"Aye, sir."

"About those personal-defense training classes you wanted to conduct down on the planet's surface?"

"Yes, sir?"

"I think now would be a good time to start arranging those."

The M'dok commander stretched lazily, purred with satisfaction, and curled up into a ball. He was comfortably fed (for the first time in how long?), pleasantly warm, and intended to sleep for the next few hours. He was on his way to doing just that when a hissing voice he knew all too well interrupted him.

"Commander! Darkness! Now would be the perfect time."

The squad leader seemed determined to sink his teeth into that afternoon's argument again, to nibble at it, worry at it, growl over it—in short, to drive the commander mad with it.

He opened one eye and bared his teeth. "Squad Leader! Orders! Now would be the perfect time for punishment for insubordination."

"But if we fail to move now, and the Federation finds us, then who will be in the wrong?"

The commander could sense the growing feeling in the others that the squad leader was right. The most elementary of battle tactics seemed to be escaping them; this plague was making them into animals. It was time to reassert himself. He rose halfway and shook himself, throwing off sleepiness, then stood erect. The commander was the tallest and broadest of the party—which was in large part why he had risen to a higher rank than any of the others. Now he glared down at them, growling as the fur along his shoulders and on his head rose, making him look even bigger. The other M'dok stepped back nervously and avoided his eyes.

He sneered, and his foot lashed out, into the pile of bones on the ground before him. Tenaran bones flew into the air and showered down on the squad leader. To have the bones of prey thrown upon him was one of the worst insults a M'dok warrior could suffer, but suffer it he did, and in silence. He had to.

The sun had set two hours earlier. On the horizon,

the moon was a thin sliver. Even for humans who lived in rural surroundings, like the Tenarans, the landscape was only dimly lighted. But to the M'dok, the light was more than adequate for killing. It had been daylight when this party had descended upon a tiny village, inhabited by only two families, and killed everyone there. Now the commander wanted to sleep until the meal was properly digested, but the squad leader wanted to keep moving, to head toward the much larger town ahead of them.

We need our minds and bodies clear before then, the commander knew.

"Enough!" he snapped. "It was I who devised the method of deceiving the satellites and thus found a way of landing on this world once again, despite the Federation defenses. I decide when we move—and where."

The squad leader, his eyes still averted, grumbled to himself, bent to pick up a human leg that still had some meat on it, and retreated behind a tree.

Satisfied, the commander dropped to the ground again, curled into a ball once more, and began to drop off to sleep. The stray thought crossed his mind that perhaps he would be wise to have the squad leader tied up until morning. But he was too sleepy and full of food to bother.

It was the first serious error the commander had ever made. It was also the last.

Chapter Nine

"ATTACK ME," Worf ordered.

Ingerment, the young Tenaran man standing in front of him, giggled. The other young Tenarans seated in a circle around the two giggled in response. Ingerment stared at the ground.

"I said, attack me!" The deep, rumbling voice was louder this time.

Ingerment giggled again, but this time with more nervousness than amusement. The others did not giggle at all. They were beginning to look uncomfortable—and some of them, scared. Still, nothing happened.

"Attack me!" Worf roared. The Tenaran turned pale, his eyes widening in fear. He raised his right hand, hesitated, and then shoved Worf lightly in the chest.

Worf raised his face to the ceiling of the gymnasium and howled the ancient cry of a Klingon warrior. The Tenarans all scrambled backward, widening the circle considerably.

Well, that didn't work. What does it take? In as mild

a tone as he could produce, Worf asked all of them, "Why can't I get any of you to truly attack me?"

A young woman spoke up angrily from the circle. "That's not the way we do things."

The others nodded in agreement.

"You said you were going to teach us how to defend ourselves against the M'dok if they attack us on the surface again, but now you want us to do the attacking!" the woman accused him.

Worf could sense their frustration and anger. Anger, he thought. We already know they're as capable of that as anyone else. Jenny de Luz found that out. So why can't they learn to control and focus that anger when needed?

"It's not that I want you to do the attacking, as you put it. I had intended to start with a demonstration of defense—my defense against your attack. That's the way I was taught self-defense, and that is the way I'm trying to teach you. When you see how easy it is for me to defend myself against you, you'll be encouraged. You'll want to learn the techniques I know."

The woman spoke again, thoughtfully this time. "It's true that a student who admires his teacher's knowledge is motivated to acquire that knowledge for himself," she pointed out to the others. "Perhaps we should try."

"Excellent," Worf said loudly. "All right, then. You." He pointed to the young woman this time, ignoring Ingerment, for he could tell that the young man was trying to avoid his eye now. "What's your name?" he asked her.

"Nadeleen."

"Nadeleen, do you have any younger brothers or sisters?"

"Three."

"Good. Do you find me frightening, Nadeleen?"

"No, not really."

"You don't?" Worf asked with some surprise.

He drew in a breath, expanding his huge chest, spread his arms out, his fingers curved into claws, and bared his teeth.

"Now?" he roared.

Nadeleen stepped back, and the circle of seated Tenarans widened again.

"Yes!"

"I'm a M'dok!" Worf yelled. "I'm attacking your family! I'm about to murder and eat your baby broth—"

That was as far as he got. Nadeleen's fist shot toward his eye. Worf was so surprised that he almost waited too long to move. Just in time, he knocked her arm aside. Still moving, he pivoted on one foot, hooked the other behind Nadeleen's legs, grabbed a handful of her blouse, and kicked her feet from under her. He used his hold on her clothes to lower her gently to the floor of the gymnasium. Even so, she was pale and shaking as she climbed to her feet. Worf smiled as unthreateningly as he could and said, "Thank you."

Ingerment said belligerently, "So what did all that mean? You were a M'dok, and she attacked you, and you knocked her down. Then you would have killed her and eaten her!"

"You weren't listening, Ingerment," Worf said. "My whole point is that I'll teach you to do what I did. That way, if I had been the Tenaran and Nadeleen had been the M'dok, I would still have been the victor. I would have had the M'dok helpless on the ground." The Tenarans looked at each other in surprised agreement. Pursuing the momentary advantage, Worf said, "Now, why don't you all get to your feet, pair off, and I'll teach you how to do what I just did to Nadeleen. There are a lot of other techniques you also need to learn, but we'll start with that one."

The rest of the afternoon went well. After some initial clumsiness and hesitation, the Tenarans began to treat the exercise as a game and took to it with increasing enthusiasm. For a while, this meant an excess of horseplay, but Worf, who was at first annoyed by it, was able to channel it in the end.

He was bone-tired when the day ended. His Tenaran students seemed, if anything, invigorated. They laughed and chatted happily and said good-bye to him cheerfully. Worf managed to maintain a friendly smile and to respond to their farewells appropriately, but behind the facade he was trembling with fatigue. He could not understand it. The physical work had been slight compared with what he was used to in his regular holodeck workouts, those martial simulations he used to keep himself in physical condition and fighting shape.

Nadeleen was the last to leave. She waited until all of the others were gone, and then she approached Worf. "I still have one big question," she announced.

Worf sighed. Naturally. Moral philosophy. Nonviolence as a way of life. "And that is?"

"Your demonstration at the beginning of the class, when you threw me to the ground. You said that showed how you could defend yourself against a M'dok. However, you know that had I been a M'dok and not a human, even if you had thrown me down hard, I'd have been back on my feet in an instant, attacking you again. They're much stronger than we are, very resilient, very aggressive. They go crazy with a kind of blood lust."

Worf mentally apologized to her. "I was going to raise that very matter tomorrow afternoon. Thank you for asking me this in private, instead of in front of the class, but I'd actually like for you to ask me the very same question tomorrow, first thing, in front of everyone else."

Nadeleen looked surprised, then agreed and walked away toward the exit. When she reached it, she paused to let two other people enter the gym first: Jenny de Luz and Gaius Aldus.

Worf greeted them with a pleased smile. "I was about to beam up. You caught me just in time."

Gaius said, "We thought you might like to come with us to see a Tenaran play, Lieutenant. Jenny and I just heard that there's one being performed here in the city this evening."

"I've been watching Tenarans play all afternoon," Worf rumbled.

Jenny laughed at the disgust in his tone. "Believe it or not, sir, this play tells about some great battle in their distant past. Or so I've been told."

Worf grunted. "Very surprising. I will attend." After a moment, he added, "Since we're both off duty and not on board ship, I'd prefer it if you'd call me Worf."

Jenny was delighted. Suddenly the forbidding Klingon warrior seemed almost human to her. She thought it wise not to tell him that, however.

The theater was much like a theater on any developed world, Worf thought. Tiers of seats for the audience faced a stage with proscenium and orchestra pit. Overhead, Worf assumed, but hidden from the audience, would be the machinery for lighting and for raising and lowering sets and equipment used for special effects.

Members of the theater crew roamed around the stage completing the setting for the opening scene. Apparently the Tenaran theater tradition did not include the use of a curtain to hide this from the audience.

As the seats filled with eager Tenarans, chatting happily with each other and waving to friends in the audience and stage crew, Worf turned to Jenny, sitting to his right, and said, "Form follows function. We could be on Earth, and it would look almost identical."

"Or Meramar," Jenny said, nodding.

Sitting on Jenny's other side, Gaius Aldus added, "Or my world. Except in Graecia, where our theater originated. The Graeci have deliberately retained the archaic format, and even give many performances in renovated theaters from ancient times. A few years ago, the old annual competition was revived in Athenae. All plays are given in the ancient language with the proper forms and costumes. Even the subject matter is drawn from their ancient mythology." He laughed. "It's almost as if the Roman conquest of Graecia had never happened. Which, I suppose," he added, "is exactly the point."

Jenny said, "Sounds a bit silly to me."

Gaius turned to her. His face was alight suddenly with a fascination Jenny had never seen there before. "Oh, no! Sometime, you must come to Athenae with me and see it for yourself. It's magnificent! No true Roman should miss it. They were our true forefathers, you know, not the primitive tribes of Latium—our cultural forebears, I mean. We fight wars our own way, and that gave us control of our world. But everything that's best in us, we got from the Graeci."

Worf knew from his reading that Gaius was expressing an opinion that the ancient Romans had held. Or tried to convince themselves was true, he corrected himself. It enabled them to think of themselves as something other than mere barbarian conquerors, which was how the Greeks really saw them.

Still, he found himself fascinated by an empire of warriors and conquerors that could give such praise to the civilization they had displaced. While Jenny and Gaius talked to each other, Worf thought: *The Klingons of the old days could never have been so generous to those they conquered. Nor could most human cultures.*

In spite of the orchestra pit, there was no music—at

least, not with this play. The stage crew simply finished setting the stage and strolled off as the actors strolled on. Worf glanced sideways and saw Jenny watching in fascination, fully prepared to enjoy the presentation. Beyond her, Gaius watched with the analytical frown of the connoisseur.

The action began. More actors came on the scene, and the stage was full of villagers discussing with concern the arrival of a band called the Lawless Ones. They shared stories about the crimes and atrocities Lawless Ones had committed in other *saavtas,* and what they might do when they arrived in theirs.

The crowd became more and more agitated and began calling for the *saavta* leader. Finally a distinguished older man arrived on the scene and settled the crowd. The leader began his speech, talking about the danger they all faced and the difficulty he had in making his decision. Finally he announced that they would fight for their *saavta,* and a stunned silence descended on the crowd, who then began murmuring their fear and disapproval.

Gaius was startled by their reaction. Certainly there was no alternative to fighting, even for the Tenarans. He watched as the leader's men devised a lottery and chose eight men, who stood before the *saavta.* The leader praised them in turn for their achievements and past contributions to their people.

The older man handed the chosen warriors weapons—either sharpened "fighting sticks" or heavy axes. He commended them again and expressed his sympathy at the loss of their honor.

Gaius started again. Surely there was no greater honor than the defense of one's people.

As the eight men were ushered out, a young girl broke from the crowd and rushed to the youngest of the warriors, a barely adolescent boy. She cried and clung tightly to him until she was finally pried away, shrieking as the warriors exited.

Then the scenery was changed quickly to indicate a forest. The eight warriors entered the stage disheveled, their clothing spotted with blood. The battle had obviously been waged and won offstage. Worf grunted his disappointment.

As the men began speaking, it became clear to Gaius that they were not making plans to return to the village. They called themselves "men without honor" and denounced themselves as murderers. Now that they had killed, they could never return to their people and would have to live alone in the forest.

Gaius watched the play's final scene with mixed emotions. He understood the importance of personal honor, as all Magna Romans did—suicide was still a common practice to restore lost honor. But for Romans, honor was inextricably bound with battle, with fighting and killing when necessary. For Tenarans, apparently, killing in self-defense meant loss of honor.

As if reading his thoughts, Worf commented, "A most curious system of honor."

Gaius nodded. Curious indeed. How could they change a people who lost their honor when they lifted a sword? And would they want to?

* * *

To Worf, food was something one consumed to keep one's body functioning optimally, not a source of pleasure. Solitary by nature, he had also found it difficult to adjust to the human habit of treating the eating of food as a central part of a larger social ritual. However, over the years he had learned to tolerate that ritual and even, occasionally, to enjoy it. Since he enjoyed the time he spent with Jenny and Gaius, when Gaius asked their opinion of the restaurant, Worf said quite honestly that it was as good as any he could remember.

Gaius was openly pleased. "Well, it's not what would be considered a feast by a patrician Roman, of course, like Captain Sejanus, but by my standards it's just fine."

"I'm surprised that the old distinction between patrician and plebeian survives in the republic," Worf said.

Gaius looked a bit embarrassed. "Not officially, no. That is, people with patrician blood don't get special favors. But unofficially, a lot of the old thinking is still around. I was brought up to consider the Volcinians, and especially Sejanus' family, as my natural masters." He laughed. "That's not in line with proper republican thinking, I know, but it's pretty deeply ingrained in some of us."

"I understand," Worf said. "Old traditions die slowly. The class structure, the warrior ethos, respect for imperial rights and privileges—it's the nature of men to adopt those ways easily and give them up with difficulty. It requires a conscious, deliberate effort." After a pause he added, "It's the nature of Klingons, as well." He noticed Jenny's surprised stare and said, "Did you believe I wasn't capable of such abstract thought, de Luz?"

Jenny looked away quickly, then back, and said, "Well, uh, some of us have wondered about you. Specifically, if you're really as different from the rest of us as you . . . Sorry."

"As I look," Worf completed for her. He felt a moment of sadness, a sense of his alienness. "Yes and no," he answered obliquely. "Nature and nurture, and the interaction of the two. I am Klingon by nature, but only part Klingon by nurture."

"My own world has a warrior heritage," Jenny said thoughtfully. "How odd that we've all ended up in Starfleet."

Gaius shrugged. "Civilizations pass beyond the need of the warrior ethos for anything but self-defense. Even Worf's people eventually reached that point."

"Now, if only the M'dok would get there," Jenny said. "And the Romulans, and all the rest of them."

"The Romulans," Gaius said thoughtfully. "They fascinated us when we first heard of them. You can understand that, I'm sure. But the more we learned about them, the less they seemed like us."

Worf nodded and added, "From what I've observed of you and the other Magna Romans, Gaius, the true similarity is between Magna Romans and Klingons."

Gaius was clearly pleased at the comparison.

Jenny said suddenly, "Then that's another thing the three of us have in common—Roman or similar origins. My ancestors were brought to Meramar by the

Preservers, just like the ancestors of the Tenarans. Except that the Tenarans apparently came from somewhere in Asia, and we came from western Hispania."

Gaius' ears pricked up at the familiar name. "During Roman times?"

"Toward the end, when the barbarians were overrunning the area. My ancestors survived for quite a while, because they were even more warlike than the barbarians who were attacking. Thanks to Servado"—she made a curious gesture over her heart with her right hand—"who took human form and organized us so that we could hold out. However, in the end there were too many of them for us, so Servado called the Preservers to take us away. Well," she added apologetically, "that's what my ancestors all believed, anyway. And then he sacrificed his mortal self in a one-man stand against the barbarians while the Preservers took away my ancestors."

"A beautiful myth," Gaius said.

Jenny stared at him angrily for a moment, until she realized that he had meant it as a compliment. "If you look at it that way," she said, feeling a bit foolish.

"The Preservers," Gaius said thoughtfully. "I wonder if we'll find them someday."

"If they still exist," Worf said. "The last trace of them is more than a thousand years old."

Gaius laughed. "To a Roman, a thousand years is the blink of an eye."

"The long view," Jenny said.

Gaius nodded. "We Romans always take the long view."

* * *

By noon, there was little left of the commander's body. The squad leader stood up, stretched, and with a smug little purr of satisfaction kicked the thick, heavy bones of his late commander, scattering them among the trees. "Now I'm in command," he announced, and no one was willing to argue with him. But they were all thinking that this new commander, like the previous one, would have to sleep eventually.

Chapter Ten

WHAT I NEED, Will Riker thought, looking out over the plains surrounding the Tenaran capital city of Zhelnogra and yawning, *is a good night's sleep.*

The last few days of traveling, and surveying settlements in the surrounding countryside, had provided him with little chance for that. And now, with the M'dok somewhere out there . . .

Well, he didn't expect things to change soon.

He and the rest of the *Enterprise*'s survey team had arrived in the capital only a few short hours ago; Riker had sent the agronomists to sleep immediately, and joined the security force patrolling the city.

It was ironic that the massive ground-based security installations and the entire satellite system they'd installed could do them absolutely no good now; the crashed M'dok ship confirmed that the satellite network, with its immensely powerful network of long- and short-range sensors, could be misled. And the ground-based part of the system, the great sensor dishes constantly sweeping the sky, had been set up to detect metal ships in space, not bodies of warm flesh on the ground.

So they had to depend on foot patrols for their security. Characteristically, the Tenaran capital city was unwalled and unguarded. Riker and his men were using hand-held tricorders, but they would be effective only once the M'dok got within range—which might be far too late.

He yawned and turned back toward the city—just as his tricorder began beeping madly.

Riker glanced at the tricorder's display screen, then quickly slapped his communicator insignia.

"Lieutenant Worf . . . I'm picking up a concentration of bodies just outside the city and heading this way."

"Understood, Commander. Sending reinforcements your way. Worf out."

Riker drew his phaser and stepped into the long prairie grass that surrounded the city.

"Who's out there?"

No answer.

"Who's out there?" Riker repeated. Now he could hear shuffling in the grass. He adjusted the settings on his phaser to heavy stun, wondering if even that would be enough to slow down a charging M'dok.

"Don't shoot!" A young man stepped into view, followed immediately by several others, including one person Riker recognized immediately.

"Gretna!" He put away his phaser and stepped forward. "Where have you been?"

She paid him no attention, striding by him as if he wasn't there.

"Wait a minute," Riker said, grabbing her arm and

spinning her around to face him. "What's the matter with you?"

"Let go of me," Gretna said, jerking her arm free.

"Keep away from her, Commander." Larten, the man from Carda who had been so rude to Riker and Gretna before, moved between the two of them and faced him threateningly.

Not wanting to provoke a confrontation, Riker took a step back. "What's he doing here?" he asked Gretna sharply. "And who are all these people?"

"I am Anka," an older woman said, stepping forward. "We are here to demand new elections to the Great *Saavta.*"

"New elections?" Riker shook his head, dumbfounded. "Gretna, what's going on?"

"Don't play innocent with me," she said, "after what Marcus told me the other night."

"What do you mean?" he asked, confused. "Marcus who?"

"Marcus Julius Volcinius. The teacher from the *Centurion.*"

"Teacher? He's no teacher." Riker shook his head. "He's Captain Sejanus' cousin—a special diplomatic envoy."

"Well, he's teaching Magna Roman history to Tenaran children," Gretna said angrily. "And don't pretend you don't know about it! Your captain—"

That was as far as she got before the screams started.

No stranger to Federation technology or to the advantage of surprise, the new M'dok commander had kept his troops close behind Gretna's party until they were well into the tall prairie grass that surrounded the city, within sight of the largest building to be seen, the Hall of the Great *Saavta*.

A few growled commands, and the horde of M'dok burst from their well-chosen concealment, moving faster than any human could possibly have run, sprinting for the building.

They ignored the Tenarans who screamed and scattered out of their way as they ran; despite their hunger, this was an elite, perfectly disciplined company. The new commander had told his troops not to deviate from the previously agreed-on plan: they were to be allowed a very brief indulgence, a bit of rest and recreation, and then they must gather their cattle, who would also serve as hostages. Finally, they would commandeer native ground transport and make for the spaceport.

One Tenaran was foolish enough to stand his ground. Tall and strong, Yavam Poroviki had been deeply impressed by the visitors from Starfleet, and had dreamed of joining it one day. *If I can do something like this, no one can deny me the chance.*

He stepped into the street, both nervous and exhilarated—but feeling more nervous by the second —as he watched the ordered formation of M'dok sprinting toward him.

"Stop!" he shouted, holding up his hand in what he hoped was an authoritative gesture. "You have no right—"

The commander understood no human language, and he wouldn't have cared if he did. The young

Tenaran's body was hurled aside with incredible force, blood gouting from his mouth as he landed. He lay quite still.

Then they were at the Hall of the Great *Saavta,* breaking formation as they jumped in through windows and doors; a few leapt onto the walls, scaling them with literally inhuman agility, to enter through openings on the second and third stories. They were all inside within seconds.

Then began a one-sided battle such as the Tenarans had never imagined in their worst nightmares.

Most of the administrative personnel within the building, generally old and completely nonviolent for all their lives, were killed without resistance as they begged for their lives. The few who tried to resist were slaughtered just as easily. Soon the walls, the furniture, and the M'doks themselves were covered with drying blood.

The famine had lasted too long, too many young and females had died, and the warriors' fury had risen too high, along with their hunger.

This slaughter was far from over.

Melkinat's office was in a relatively isolated wing on the third floor, so it took some time for the noise of the battle to reach him. When it did, he looked up from his paperwork, shook his head, and tried to dismiss it, until the sound became too loud to ignore.

He set down his pen and listened, with irritation, and then, growing fear. At first it had sounded like workmen; now, as he listened more closely, it seemed that he could hear screams and growls, and other noises he didn't even want to begin identifying.

Suddenly very afraid, he rose from his desk, the candles casting a flickering shadow of him upon the wall. His shadow looked larger than he was. *Is this what I've become? A shadow?*

No!

For the first time in years, he looked at himself. He had never been especially tall; it was his powerful orator's voice, not his physical presence, which had made him such a successful politician. Though he was growing old, he was still strong—the years of hard work on his family's farm having left their mark on his muscles. His appearance of frailty was just an appearance, not reality. Now, after decades, he realized that he was not a weak old man, but a powerful one—and, therefore, potentially dangerous.

His peers on the Central Council would have been surprised to see the grin that appeared on his lips then—a hard, dangerous smile, the tips of his teeth showing from beneath thin lips. With a single stride— and how good it felt to walk again, instead of shuffling!—he was at the opposite wall, lifting the great ax from the brackets that held it. Then he opened his door and ran out into the corridor.

There was blood splattered on the wall.

A M'dok warrior stood there, and clenched in each paw was a Tenaran. Melkinat could no longer recognize the faces, but he was quite sure that he had known both those men.

With a shout that drowned the warrior's growl, he

rushed at the great cat, swinging the ax two-handed. The M'dok was more than a bit surprised to find a Tenaran who actually fought, and he hesitated for a fraction of a second. That brief hesitation cost him his life.

Just as the M'dok was beginning to move, the keen steel sliced deep into his side, crushing both the inner and outer set of ribs. Melkinat tightened his grip on the haft as he felt the force of the impact run up his forearms.

He pulled the ax free, and the M'dok commander crumpled, blood spilling out across the floor.

Melkinat stared down into its eyes, and what he saw there suddenly sickened him.

The creature was in agony.

The M'dok shuddered once and lay still.

Merciful God, Melkinat thought in silent shock, standing there over the body, fighting the urge to vomit. *A living being—and I killed it.*

Yes, and I will kill many more, and I will go on killing until my world is safe. He knew something fundamental had changed inside him, and it would never change back again.

He turned to go down the stairs, toward the sounds of battle below, ax in hand.

Gretna watched Will Riker's face closely as he listened to the disembodied voice coming over his communicator.

"They're inside the Great Hall, Commander. Ensign de Luz reports heavy fighting. I'm on my way there now."

"I'll be there quick as I can, Worf. Riker out." He turned back to the Tenarans.

"The M'dok are attacking the city. Stay here, and stay together. You should be safe."

With those words he was off and running. He was fifty feet from the entrance to the Great Hall before he realized Gretna was following him.

"What are you doing?" he yelled, coming to a stop.

"My father could be in there!" Gretna said. "And if he is, his life's in danger!"

Horrendous sounds of battle, of screaming and yowling, and phasers firing, could be heard from within.

"In danger?" Will bent over to catch his breath. "Did I ever tell you how perceptive you are for a naive Tenaran girl?"

Gretna tried hard not to smile, but failed.

"Will," she began. "I—"

The front door to the Great Hall flew open, and a M'dok warrior sprang out at them.

Will had no time to draw his phaser. He simply threw himself in front of Gretna, and met the charging M'dok head-on. The two of them fell to the ground, the M'dok's yowling mixing with Riker's shouts.

Gretna screamed. "Will!"

Riker fell silent. The M'dok gained its feet, and stood poised over him, its claws unsheathed to strike.

Simultaneously, a beam of light shot out of the doorway and struck the M'dok. It crumpled to the ground and lay still.

A tall alien in a Starfleet uniform, almost as

fearsome-looking as the M'dok, stepped out of the doorway.

"Are you all right?" he asked Gretna.

"I'm fine, but Will . . ."

The alien knelt by Riker's side and turned him over. He took one look and slapped his communicator.

"Worf to sick bay . . . Emergency! Beam Commander Riker aboard immediately!"

When he lifted his hand off the communicator, blood stained his uniform.

"Will he be all right?" Gretna asked.

Worf nodded hesitantly. "Yes. His injuries do not seem severe."

She turned back toward the Great Hall. The fighting within seemed to have stopped. "I've got to find my father."

"Wait," Worf said.

Gretna turned.

"You are Gretna Melkinata?"

"I am."

"Your father is not in there." Worf hesitated. "I regret to tell you he is already aboard the *Enterprise*. He is very seriously injured."

Just outside Zhelnogra, where the city disappeared into prairie that had remained unchanged for a length of time beyond understanding, the burial party was hard at work.

Jenny de Luz, Lieutenant Worf, and a few Tenaran survivors were digging graves for those who had fallen in the attack on the city. In places, the giant sensor dishes of the defense system rose above the prairie, metal gleaming in the midst of the tall grass. *The system was perfectly set up,* Jenny thought. *And yet it failed miserably. And I'm the one who certified that the satellite web was complete and sufficient. I am responsible for much of what happened.*

She straightened briefly, breathing in the cold, clean air, stretching her weary back. A few hundred yards distant, Worf continued digging, working at a relentless pace.

Gaius had beamed back scant minutes ago to the *Centurion,* to tend to one of his own men injured in the attack.

Luckily, none of the *Enterprise* personnel (save Commander Riker, of course) on the surface had been caught in the attack—only the Tenarans. And many more of them would have lived, had they bothered to pay attention to Worf's self-defense lessons.

She started to bend back to her work, then stopped; her trained ears had caught the sound of a transporter beam. Then she discerned the approaching figure more clearly, and stiffened in surprise; the man walking toward her, his cloak of dark purple swirling about him as he strode across the dusty field as though he walked the polished floor of the Roman imperial court, was Captain Lucius Aelius Sejanus.

Reflexively Jenny stiffened to attention.

With a little half-smile the captain said, "Be at ease, Ensign." He laid a hand on her shoulder. "Gaius told me how upset you were over this attack. I came down to make sure you were all right."

"I'm fine, sir. Just a little . . . frustrated."

Sejanus eyed her questioningly. "Frustrated?"

"Yes." Jenny's normally timid voice filled with anger. "Had the security teams been there earlier—indeed, had the Tenarans themselves accepted our offers to arm them—we could easily have prevented this."

Sejanus nodded. "Go on."

"The Tenarans are weak, Captain Sejanus," Jenny said angrily, all the frustration of the last few weeks eating at her. "They will not arm themselves, they cannot fight, they . . ." Words failed her, and she finished the declaration with a weak gesture.

"I share your concern, Ensign," Sejanus replied. "But perhaps they can be protected, so long as you and your personnel perform as valiantly as you did today."

"Thank you, sir."

He eyed her carefully a moment before speaking again. "And perhaps there are other measures we can take as well."

"Sir?" Jenny asked, slightly confused.

Sejanus' communicator chirped.

"Excuse me a moment." He touched his insignia. "Sejanus here. Go ahead."

"Captain, we have just received word from the *Enterprise*. Chairman Melkinat is dead."

"Oh, no," Jenny said, the shovel slipping out of her hands.

Sejanus' face turned grave. "Thank you, Lieutenant. Hold one moment." He turned back to Jenny. "I must go . . . but I would like to continue our conversation. The next time you are aboard the *Centurion* . . . ?"

Jenny almost blushed. She was planning to beam up there later this evening to see Gaius, after her work on the surface was completed. But there was no need to tell Captain Sejanus that. "I will be aboard tomorrow morning, sir."

"Excellent," Sejanus said. "Come talk to me then." He bowed, then reached up to tap his communicator. "Sejanus to *Centurion*. One to beam up."

It was a long time before Jenny could concentrate her thoughts enough to go back to work.

Chapter Eleven

Captain's Log, Stardate 41800.9:

I have just returned from a very disturbing session with the remaining officials of Tenara's Great *Saavta*.

The death of Chairman Melkinat has shaken the whole government to its core. They are now calling for the removal of all Federation forces, and that call is being led by Gretna Melkinata—the late chairman's daughter. Up until a week ago, I would have counted on her support for a continued Federation presence here to help the Tenarans defend their world. I am at a loss to explain her actions— while Commander Riker, who knew her best of all, remains unconscious in sick bay, recovering from wounds received during the latest attack by the M'dok.

There is one encouraging piece of news in all this, however. The M'dok we have captured bear out Commander Data's hypothesis of famine in the empire. We have dispatched this information to Starfleet, who are bringing increased diplomatic pressure to bear. In the meantime, the situation

here remains explosive. I feel that Captain Sejanus
and *Centurion* are merely waiting for the M'dok to
reappear to start a full-scale war.

PICARD SIGHED AND LEANED BACK in his chair, shutting
off the log recorder.

"Quite a day, sir," Deanna Troi said.

"Indeed, Counselor. And it's only morning." He
put a finger to his lips and rubbed them thoughtfully.
"I wish I could talk to Commander Riker about all
this." He flipped a toggle on his chair, opening a
channel to sick bay. "Dr. Crusher, how's our patient?"

"He's lost a lot of blood, Captain." Beverly Crusher's voice came back. "But he's coming along nicely."

"I need to talk to him."

"And he needs to sleep. At least another twenty-
four hours."

The determination in her voice was clear. Picard
gritted his teeth. "Very well, Doctor. Keep me in-
formed."

He turned his attention to the main viewscreen,
dominated by Tenara and the *Centurion*.

*Much more than I need to talk to Commander Riker,
I need to talk to the captain of that ship. To find out
what he's thinking, what he plans to do next.*

And he might as well be a million miles away.

The door to Sejanus' quarters slid open, and Ensign
Jenny de Luz stepped inside. Sejanus was waiting for
her, standing beside a desk. He was wearing a simple
Starfleet uniform just like that worn by Jean-Luc
Picard; it made his similarity to the *Enterprise* captain

all the more striking, even uncanny. He smiled with pleasure and came forward to take her hand in greeting. "Ensign de Luz. Welcome to my ship. May I call you Jenny?"

"Yes, Captain. Of course."

Sejanus released her hand and walked over to the windows and stood looking at Tenara spinning lazily below them. "I've been monitoring your holodeck exercises." He turned back to her and smiled. "Your scores are most impressive."

"It's thanks to Gaius, sir."

"You're too modest, Jenny. He tells me everything —and he tells me you're one of the most promising young officers he's come across in years. Even including the Magna Romans. But then, there's a little bit of Rome in your background, isn't there?"

Jenny smiled. "Actually, sir, only partly. Most of my ancestors were the native peoples conquered by the Romans."

"The same may well be true of me," Sejanus said with a laugh. "I've never been convinced that the Volcinians, or any of the other gentis who claim to trace their ancestry back to the original Roman patrician families, have kept their bloodlines as pure through the centuries as we like to tell ourselves." He seated himself on the edge of the desk. "I was brought up believing that all of that—ancestry, purity of blood—was more important than anything else. I believed every detail of it. But for years I've struggled to overcome that upbringing. First I tried to make myself see that I had to think in terms of my whole world, of all Magna Romans, and not just of Romans.

Then I tried to expand my view still further, to embrace all the member peoples of the Federation."

"Yes, sir." Jenny nodded. "That's just what I had to learn when I left Meramar. That's what Captain Picard says quite often."

"Does he?" Sejanus cleared his throat. "Your captain is a great man. He's famous throughout Starfleet and the Federation, and justly so. A scholar, a soldier when necessary, a diplomat, a leader—yes, he deserves his fame. I can certainly understand why his crew admire him."

"We do, sir."

Sejanus nodded. "And I'm sure that Captain Picard's real concern is for the good of the peoples and worlds that make up the Federation."

"I'm sure of that too, sir."

Sejanus raised his eyes to meet hers. "But, Jenny, it's important not to be blinded by hero worship. Even Jean-Luc Picard is capable of making mistakes."

"Of . . . of course, sir. I'm sure he'd be the first to agree."

Sejanus nodded. "I'm sure you're right," he said seriously. "That's partly a measure of the man's greatness—that he's willing to admit that he's as fallible as anyone else. Unfortunately, that doesn't mean that he's always able to see where he's going wrong, even if it's pointed out to him. He may wish for the best for the Federation, but he may not be taking the best approach to ensuring the Federation's health."

Suddenly Jenny began to feel confused. "I don't know what you mean, Captain."

Sejanus stood slowly. "Let me give you some background to the Battle of Britannia. No, I'm not changing the subject. You'll see; it's relevant. Do you know why the German tribes put aside their differences and undertook an expedition to Britannia to attack Londinium?"

"Gaius told me they thought it was undefended, that the legions had been withdrawn."

"Yes, but why did they think that?"

Jenny shook her head. "I didn't ask."

His voice turned crisp and authoritative. "Like the Romans of Earth, my ancestors tried unsuccessfully to conquer the Germans. We lost untold numbers of men in those forests, and we scarcely gained any ground.

"But we noticed that the Germans were becoming more like us! They resisted us as conquerors, but between fights, they traded with the Roman settlements along their borders, they learned Latin, they learned to emulate our forms of government and military organization. If anything, we realized that this made them an even greater threat to us. But it also pointed the way to a different method of conquest.

"So we started sending in teachers and traders instead of soldiers. The first few were slaughtered, of course, but eventually the Germans let them survive and stay. Bit by bit, our culture, our civilization, was bringing about the conquest that our armies had failed to achieve.

"And then a revivalist movement started in Germania—cultural revival, nationalism, rejecting everything foreign, which is to say, Roman. Within two years they had dismantled everything we had built, killed or imprisoned all of our people, and terrified all the Romanized Germans into returning to primitive ways. Food, language, housing, the arts—everything became primitive again. And we were back where we had started centuries before.

"Then we realized that we were even worse off than we had been. The new leaders of Germania were cooperating with each other, and they were more aware than before of our empire as a threat. Our spies discovered that they were trying to organize an invasion of the empire, with Rome itself as their goal.

"Our first impulse was to organize as large an army as we could and send it north into Germania to crush them once and for all. But the Emperor Belisarius feared that his legions would simply be slaughtered in the forest, as had happened centuries earlier. He and his generals hit upon a brilliant strategy. They sent couriers through Germania, on one of the shorter routes toward Britannia, carrying secret messages to the legions in Britannia."

"But that seems very foolish," Jenny protested. "They might have been captured."

Sejanus grinned. "They were. And they were tortured and killed, and their messages were translated. The messages were orders that the legions withdraw to Italia to help repel the expected German invasion. The true orders, that the legions were to stay where they were, were sent to Britannia by sea, along with many reinforcements. The Germans fell for the ruse and sent the cream of their forces to attack what they thought was unguarded Britannia. They thought to eat away at the empire from the edges, but instead they fell into a perfect trap, as you saw on the holodeck. The aftermath was that Germania was denuded of its defensive forces, and Emperor Belisarius then sent his legions in and conquered all of Germania in a brilliant campaign taking only three months."

"That was a very risky trick," Jenny pointed out.

"Yes, but it worked, and that's what really counts, isn't it?"

"Would those couriers think so, Captain? I mean, the ones who were sent across Germania with fake messages? You said they were caught and tortured and killed."

"They were Romans, Jenny. They knew the risk, and they accepted it as part of their duty." He paused. "Perhaps you're beginning to see my point, why I told you this whole story about the background to the Battle of Britannia. What saved Britannia and the rest of the empire was the willing self-sacrifice of brave Romans. A direct approach—a brute-force invasion of Germania—would have failed. It might even have led to the downfall of the empire. There might be no Magna Roma today. And that's really my point. That's what I want you to think about."

Jenny shook her head, confused. "I'm afraid I still don't understand what you're getting at."

Sejanus now turned his back on her and began pacing across the ready room. "What I'm getting at, Jenny, is that what your captain is doing now—here, on Tenara—is a mistake." He turned to face her. "It's cost the lives of dozens of Tenarans, and it will cost the lives of many more people—from this ship and yours, I would say—before Picard will admit his mistake."

"With all due respect, sir, that's something you should take up with him, not me."

Sejanus laughed. He walked over to Jenny and put his hands on her shoulders. "I can understand Gaius' interest in you. He has chosen exceptionally well."

His voice vibrated through her. Jenny stepped away, breaking the contact. "Thank you, sir."

Sejanus turned toward the window and studied the stars outside. He waited a moment before speaking again. "I remember your words on the surface of Tenara, Jenny—how you felt the deaths there were unnecessary. Do you remember mine?"

Jenny nodded. "You said there were other measures we could take to ensure the Tenarans' safety."

"Exactly," Sejanus said. He turned back to her, his eyes alight with excitement.

"The time has come to take those other measures, Jenny. To strike back at the enemies of the Federation, to do something bold, something daring, something that will do more to ensure the long-term safety of our worlds and peoples than any number of defensive outposts we could ever set up!" He gripped her shoulders again, and stared into her eyes. "Something that will require brave followers of the old Roman mold, followers unafraid to sacrifice their lives for what they believe is right.

"Jenny," Sejanus drew her closer. "I think you are of that mold—I know Gaius Aldus does. We want you here, aboard the *Centurion,* to help in that undertaking."

"I . . ." Jenny chose her words carefully. "Captain, it may happen that I'll be requesting a transfer to the *Centurion* in the future anyway. I've been thinking that I ought to speak to you about it, to make sure you'd approve the request."

"Approve!" Sejanus fairly shouted. "Jenny, I'd be delighted. I want officers who can think on their feet, react quickly—above all, officers unafraid to do what has to be done. People like you, Jenny."

She drew a shaky breath. "Thank you, sir. Then I would be honored to serve under your command."

"Excellent, Jenny." He clapped his hands. "Why don't you speak to your captain? And I'll make all the necessary arrangements here."

"Yes, sir."

Sejanus nodded, and watched her go. The two members of his personal guard who had been standing outside his door would escort her safely back to the transporter room—or to Gaius' quarters, wherever she wanted to go.

Of course, had Jenny balked at his offer, or behaved even the slightest bit suspiciously, he would have had them escort her someplace else entirely.

It was much easier this way.

Deanna Troi was not surprised when Jenny asked for a counseling session so soon after the M'dok attack; she was, however, surprised by what Jenny wanted to tell her.

"A transfer, Jenny? Why?"

"Maybe I'm just tired of not fitting in here, Deanna.

On the *Centurion,* I feel I belong. They're all warriors there, like I am!"

"Jenny . . ." Deanna shook her head. "I know how fond you are of Gaius, how much you feel a part of the *Centurion.* That's all wonderful. But you need to get one thing very clear in your own mind. Starfleet is not an organization of warriors. We fight when we have to, yes, but—"

"But we have to fight now! After what happened yesterday, isn't our obligation to pursue the M'dok to their homeworld and destroy their ability to wage war?" Jenny asked. "Rid the Galaxy of the threat they pose! The same applies to any other enemy that threatens any of our worlds. Why shouldn't we really train the Tenarans to defend themselves, force them to change their society so that they'll be safe even when our two ships leave? After all, no enemy in his right mind would attack Magna Roma or Meramar. We should insist that the Tenarans be able to fight for themselves—shouldn't we?"

"Isn't that a choice for the Tenarans to make?" Deanna asked carefully.

Jenny's hand cut the air like a weapon. It was more than an aggressive gesture; it betrayed suppressed nervous tension and energy. "Not if they're going to keep on asking the rest of us to protect them from attack! They're using us as their shield so that they can have the luxury of living the way they want to."

As Jenny spoke, Deanna listened to her words, and at the same time she listened to her feelings. The empathic sense Deanna derived from the Betazoid half of her told her that Jenny was being torn in two.

This was more than an intellectual argument she was having with herself, an internal debate about two conflicting value systems; this was a fundamental split, a tear in her being.

"Jenny, I can't decide questions of political philosophy for you. You have to do that for yourself. Every adult, every citizen of the Federation, has the duty to do just that. I'm here to help you with your problems of emotional adjustment. I don't—"

"That is my problem!" Jenny cried. "Everything I believed in is coming apart! Can't you tell?"

Yes, Deanna thought, *of course I can tell. But I still can't prescribe an answer for you.* "Jenny, I think you could use a bit of a break from your work before you decide to transfer to the *Centurion.* One way or another."

"All right," Jenny said dully. "With Lieutenant Worf down there, they really don't need me at all."

"Good. I'll get permission from the captain for you to get some time off, and then I'll want to see you again after that. In the meantime, here's what I want you to do. I know you had sections in your Academy history courses on fascism and English common law."

Jenny nodded. She seemed suddenly spent, as if her furious outburst had used up all her strength.

"I don't feel that they cover either subject in enough detail," Deanna said. "I want you to spend your days off reading as much of what the computer has on those two topics as you can manage. All right?"

"All right."

Deanna patted her on the shoulder. "I'll speak to you later."

"Thank you, Counselor."

When Deanna Troi left, Jenny threw herself onto her bed and stared up at the painting on her cabin wall. She had brought it with her from Meramar—the only keepsake she'd allowed herself from her native world. It was a rendition of Servado's Agony: the semidivine hero crucified by the barbarian horsemen he had held off single-handedly for so long. Below the rough cross, Servado's sword lay broken in two. Despite the nails through his palms, the crown of thorns on his head, and the lance wound in his side, Servado gazed out of the painting with inhuman calm. His eyes held a message that Jenny had treasured all her life: "Be courageous, my daughter. Be a warrior in my image, and we will meet in heaven."

The message that tradition said was the last he had spoken in this world was written across the bottom of the painting: *"Resorgo."* In the language of Meramar this meant, "I shall rise again." It was Servado's promise to his people.

Beneath the painting was a small altar covered with a white cloth. A plain sword lay on it, much like those produced for generations in Hispania by Jenny's ancestors for the legions of Rome. Straight, two-edged, unadorned, it was a slender, lightweight version of the legionary's sword. Jenny, dressed in white, knelt before the altar.

"Holy Servado," she whispered, "bless my weapon and my undertaking. Be with me as you were with my father. Show me the right way."

She looked up at the painting hanging above her. Servado's gaze looked as stern and loving and approving as it always did, but now she thought she saw something else there as well. Something she had seen in Sejanus' eyes too.

"Holy Servado," she whispered. "Did you reappear after all on another world?"

But there was no reply. She bent her head again and continued to pray, sometimes in English, sometimes in her native language—that corrupted, convoluted tongue that had once been Latin.

Chapter Twelve

IT WAS TRULY BEYOND BELIEF.

Three days had passed since the M'dok attack. Worf had even more people in the self-defense classes he was organizing than before—so many, in fact, that he had requested Gaius Aldus' help in teaching the class. The Magna Roman, who had yet to arrive this afternoon, was an expert in unarmed combat as well—and much easier for the Tenarans to relate to, Worf had to admit.

And still the Tenarans found reasons not to defend themselves.

As Worf had asked her to, Nadeleen repeated the objection she had made to him in private three days ago. "I am glad you asked that question," Worf said. He had the full attention of the class.

"Because you are quite right, Nadeleen. A M'dok warrior would have sprung back to his feet and attacked again. Your counterattack must be swift enough, powerful enough, that the M'dok is no longer able to get up. That is what I will teach you today."

He picked a young girl at random from the crowd.

"You—what is your name?"

"Arkanka, sir."

"Very well, Arkanka, please come here."

She stood up and approached him warily. Arkanka was a couple of years younger than Nadeleen, but she was as tall as Worf and looked strong enough. *Against the M'dok, she would have a fighting chance—if she learns what I teach*.

"Now," Worf told the group, "there are various parts of the body where humanoids, even M'dok, are particularly vulnerable to serious injury. Blows struck there, hard enough, done properly, can even cause death."

The Tenarans all shivered simultaneously. Engrossed in his lecture, Worf didn't notice the movement. "We will pass over most of them for two reasons. First, I'm trying to keep what I teach you pared down to the essentials and avoid more advanced details. And second, you would be foolish to try for most of those places on a M'dok. The exception, however, is the throat.

"When the M'dok attack, they do so with their arms out, so that they can strike with their talons, and their heads up so that they can bite downward. They expect their prey to be terrified, frozen with fear, so they don't worry about the fact that their own throats are exposed. They are therefore vulnerable to the few simple strikes I will now teach you. Arkanka, put your arms out and your head up. Like this." Worf posed for her.

"Just a minute!" Arkanka objected. "Are you saying that you're going to teach us how to deliberately injure someone?"

"Not 'someone.' An attacker. Presumably, a M'dok warrior."

The whispers changed to angry mutters.

"We can't do that," Arkanka said firmly.

"Can't . . ." Worf took a deep breath and tried again. "I do not think any of you will use what I teach you to attack an innocent person. We're discussing self-defense, remember."

"Even so," Ingerment said, "we thought it would be all right, because you showed us how to defend ourselves without hurting the other person. But now you're talking about something unacceptable."

"Unacceptable?" Worf repeated. "Is it unacceptable to do what you have to do to save yourself? It will take more than simple judo throws to stop the M'dok."

"Then we won't stop them." Some of them stood and began to walk toward the exit.

Before a general movement could develop, Worf said, "Explain that to me, please."

Ingerment looked at the others, and seeing that they accepted him as their spokesman, went on. "We'd rather let them hurt us than be forced to hurt them in order to stop them."

"'Hurt'? M'dok do not 'hurt,'" Worf pointed out. "They kill."

"All right, then," Ingerment said stubbornly. "We'd rather let them kill us than be forced to kill them."

"Better to die than be forced to take on the moral stain of murder," Arkanka added.

Worf said, "But if one of you is going to die

anyway—you or the M'dok—isn't it better if it's the M'dok?"

"Why is a M'dok less worthy of living than we are?" Nadeleen asked. "We're all sentients, so what's the difference?"

Worf thought a moment. "I like Tenarans a lot more than I like M'dok." That earned him a few smiles, but he could see that the issue had not gone away. "What about Nadeleen's reaction the other day? What if it is not your own life at stake, but the life of a child or someone else unable to defend himself?"

Ingerment had an answer for that. "They'd also prefer to die rather than force any of us to commit murder to protect them. Every Tenaran feels that way."

"Every Tenaran?" Worf asked. "Even Melkinat, who took down an ancient weapon from the wall and split a M'dok skull when the M'dok attacked Zhelnogra?"

"We're as capable of an irrational reaction as any other sentient being," Nadeleen answered him quietly. "But that doesn't mean that it's proper to react that way. Our laws and customs are based on reason, not irrational rage."

Worf shook his head. "I respect your beliefs—if every sentient in the Galaxy behaved the way you do, there'd be peace everywhere. But you've seen that the Galaxy doesn't work that way. You have to deal with reality, not theory."

"We are dealing with reality," Nadeleen said. "You're the one who's fooling himself, finding excuses to give free rein to his bloodthirsty instincts. We won't let you pollute our world with any of that." She stood up and walked rapidly toward the exit.

The others followed her. Worf called after them, but they ignored him. Their unwillingness to fight infuriated him.

Behind him, he heard laughter.

He spun around. Walking toward him across the gymnasium floor was a young man dressed in a Roman toga edged with purple and wearing sandals worked with silver and gold thread. Worf was annoyed with himself that he had not noticed this man— presumably a Magna Roman—before, and even more annoyed at the laughter, which he took to be directed at him. He stiffened and waited silently for the other man to come up to him.

The young man raised a hand in greeting. "I'm Marcus Julius Volcinius, and of course I know who you are." He became aware at last of Worf's lack of response to his greetings. "Oh, forgive me," Marcus said quickly. "I wasn't laughing at you! I was laughing at . . . at the irony of your undertaking."

"Irony?" Worf rumbled.

"Oh, yes. You're trying to undo a lifetime of training with a few hours' instruction." He shook his head. "Doomed before you start."

Worf gestured toward the door through which the last of the Tenarans had exited. "They're all young still. I chose them for that."

"Ah, but not young enough! How soon does a Roman become a Roman, or a Klingon a Klingon?"

"Klingons have a rite of passage," Worf said cautiously, "after which one is deemed an adult."

Marcus nodded. "Of course, of course. All societies invent such rituals. That's not what I'm talking about. I asked you at what age a child becomes imbued with the values of its society."

"That depends on the child—and the society."

Marcus grinned widely. "Spoken more like a diplomat than a warrior. However, it's clear to me that the younger one gets the children, the better the chance of changing their development."

Worf frowned. "You mean more than you're saying. Please explain."

"Hmm. Yes. A Roman habit—to mean much more than we say."

"A habit this snake is excellent at." Gaius Aldus had approached silently, and now stood behind Marcus. "I was delayed aboard ship, Lieutenant, but I see our class has left us already."

"More problems over what constitutes self-defense, Gaius," Worf said. "Marcus Julius, I think, was going to suggest a solution to our problem."

"Were you, now, Marcus?"

"Gaius," Marcus said, bowing slightly. "A pleasure to see you again."

"And for me as well, Marcus Julius, though I am surprised to see you down here. You should be aboard the *Centurion*, where you can't get in anyone's way." His arm shot out, and he grabbed Marcus by the wrist. "What are you doing here?"

Marcus twisted free, bruising his arm in the process. "You don't know everything that goes on, Gaius."

Gaius drew himself up. "I'm supposed to know everything important. I'm the *magister navis*."

Marcus laughed at him. "You shouldn't take archaic titles too seriously."

"All right, Marcus. Don't take my title seriously." He grabbed Marcus' arm again, and dragged him closer. "Take *me* seriously. Now, what are you doing here?"

Marcus looked down at the powerful hand gripping his arm. This time, he could tell, Gaius would not let his hold be thrown off easily, and Marcus had no wish to make a fool of himself by struggling ineffectually against Gaius in the street.

Besides, it would give him pleasure to show the *"magister navis"* how out of touch with reality he truly was. "I'll show you," he said. "Come with me."

"Excuse us, Lieutenant," Gaius said. "I will speak to you later."

"Of course," Worf said.

Marcus led the way to a small one-story building divided into two rooms. Both were being used as classrooms, and both were filled with Tenaran children, sitting attentively at desks arranged in rows, being taught by Magna Romans dressed as Marcus was—although without the purple edging to their togas or the silver and gold stitching on their sandals.

Marcus smiled at the look of shock on Gaius' face as he passed by the open doors of both classrooms.

"By the gods, Marcus, you've gone too far," he said through clenched teeth. "You have no authority to assign these personnel here."

Marcus said nothing, merely nodded through an open door at one of the classes. In answer to a question from the teacher, a boy of about six slid from his desk, jumped to his feet, stood at military attention, and recited, *"Nomen Romanum* refers to the Roman power, which is supreme all over the world of Magna Roma."

"Very good, Tullius," the teacher said. The teacher was a middle-aged woman, very erect, very patrician. "You may sit down."

Tullius smiled happily and sat in his desk again, like all the other children sat, erect, stiff-backed.

The teacher called on another child. "Antonia, finish this sentence for me, and then translate it into Tenaran: *'Roma locutaest . . .'"*

A little girl, no older than five, jumped to her feet and stood just as stiffly as her classmate Tullius had and said in a singsong, *"Roma locuta est; causa finita est.* It means, 'Rome has spoken; the case is ended.'"

"Excellent, Antonia. Anyone, what does that really mean?"

Gaius turned away.

"Come," Marcus said. "There's more."

Now he led the way behind the building. There a high wall blocked their way. It also protected whatever it enclosed from observation. The wall was made of the same metal used aboard starships for interior walls.

"The Tenarans build with stone and wood," Gaius said.

"Correct. We added the wall ourselves, for privacy."

As if to emphasize the off-planet origin of the wall, the door set into it stayed closed until Marcus said to it, *"Aperi!"* At his command, the door slid to one side, admitted the two men, and then slid shut behind them. Beyond the door was a flat space entirely surrounded by the wall. On that dusty field, Roman troops were drilling.

"From the ship?"

Marcus grinned. "Look again."

Gaius did. The trainees were boys and girls, of whom the oldest was fifteen or sixteen. Then it struck him. "Tenarans!"

Marcus laughed in delight. "Exactly! Young Tenarans! And they take to it, Gaius, they take to it! Watch them."

Before them, the ranks dressed in archaic Roman armor and armed with ancient Roman weapons marched and wheeled and turned in response to shouted orders—always in Latin—from a Magna Roman officer. At his order they stopped with a simultaneous ground-shaking tramp of booted feet. Another yell in Latin, and they all turned to face Gaius and Marcus, struck their fists to their chests, and then shot out their arms in a Roman salute. In one voice they cried out, *"Salvete!"*

Gaius turned and stalked back to the door. When it didn't open for him, he said, "Open!" There was no response. He tried the same command in Latin, imitating Marcus: *"Aperi!"* Still there was no response.

Behind him, Marcus chuckled. "It's not set to recognize your voice, Lieutenant."

Without turning, Gaius said quietly, but in a

deep rumble that carried across the parade ground, "Then open it for me, or I'll break my way through it."

"I'm planting seeds. We're doing this all over the planet. In time, these children will reach the age when they begin to play a role in shaping the destiny of Tenara. Some of them will enter the *saavtas*. Others will create a native armed force."

"An armed force?"

Marcus nodded. His eyes shone with pride. "Modeled after the Roman legions. They won't need our help to repel attack the next time. More important, however, they and their comrades in the *saavtas* will . . ." He paused, searching for the right phrase. "They will alter the nature of this world and perhaps the Federation as well."

"Marcus, you fool." Gaius shook his head sadly. "I don't know where you got the idea for this, but it stops now. You'll dismantle your schools immediately, and you will return to the ship and bring all of your teachers with you."

Marcus shook his head. "You still don't understand, do you? I'm not under your command. I'm Sejanus' cousin, I'm here at his invitation, and I take my orders from him. What I'm doing now, in fact, is by his orders. Furthermore, if I were a plebe like you, I'd be more careful. Life can be most uncomfortable for those who insult members of certain families—even in these democratic, republican days."

"The captain would never approve of what you've done."

"Do you really think so, Gaius?"

"We'll see what Lucius Aelius Sejanus has to say about this!" Gaius slapped his communicator. *"Centurion!* One to beam up, and be quick about it!"

When Gaius Aldus materialized on the platform of the *Centurion's* transporter room, the technician standing behind the console instantly straightened to attention and slapped his fist to his chest, then snapped his arm out, hand straight, palm down, in the ancient Roman salute.

Gaius did not even notice. He leapt from the platform and rushed from the room, down the corridor to the nearest turbolift. He ignored greetings and salutes from those he passed. He was unaware of the people along the way. He was preoccupied with what he'd seen on the surface of Tenara, and what it implied.

Marcus, of course, was right: Gaius was a plebe. In the old days, that would have meant that he was nothing, that his family name meant nothing, that he was not considered to have such a thing as honor. In these times, he was still unimportant and his family name still meant nothing. But now he had honor, and he would protect it. It was all he had—except for Jenny.

In his quarters, Gaius used the communicator screen on his desk to contact his captain. The computer found Sejanus in his ready room, busy with some of the mundane details that running a starship required. He looked annoyed at being interrupted, but brightened somewhat when he saw who was calling him.

"Gaius! What are you doing on board? Aren't you supposed to be helping that *Enterprise* security team with—"

"Captain," Gaius broke in. "I need to see you. Immediately."

Sejanus frowned. "I'm rather bogged down at the moment. Can it wait until this evening?"

"I'm afraid not, Captain."

Sejanus nodded, instantly serious at the undertone in his first officer's voice. "Then come immediately. The ready room."

The communications screen went dark.

Gaius sighed and pulled off his Starfleet uniform. Slowly, and with great care, he put on his dress uniform, reserved only for ceremonial occasions. This had changed little since ancient times; it was the garb of the Magna Romans who had set out to conquer a world—and succeeded. First came a tunic. Over that, he put on a heavy breastplate with armored epaulets. He added a skirt onto which plates of metal armor had been sewn, a helmet, and a cloak. Finally he strapped to his waist a belt from which dangled a short, broad sword—ceremonial, but sharp-pointed and edged.

He examined himself in the full-length mirror set upon one wall. He adjusted his armor, hiked up his sword belt, and then, satisfied, stood to attention and gave his image the Roman salute.

Now he felt ready for what was required of him. Gaius left his quarters and headed for the bridge.

Once again, the crew members Gaius passed saluted him. Before, they had done so because they respected him and because of his high status on the ship. Now they did so for both of those reasons and also because of the ancient, revered uniform he wore. And this time, Gaius walked more slowly, noticed the salutes, and returned them gravely. *"Salve,"* he said quietly. *"Salve."*

The turbolift doors slid open, and Gaius Aldus stepped onto the bridge, the embodiment of *Roma Aeterna,* Eternal Rome. Conversation on the bridge stopped, and the crew watched in fascination as Gaius walked across the bridge with great dignity and entered the ready room.

As the door slid shut behind him, Sejanus looked up from his desk. "Gaius. Be welcome." Then the uniform registered on him, and he raised his eyebrows. "Such ceremony with me, Gaius?"

"Captain, you paid me the compliment of telling Jean-Luc Picard that I have long protected your honor as well as your life."

Sejanus nodded. "Quite true. Not a compliment, but the simple truth."

"Then it is my duty to warn you that that honor is in great danger."

"I'm not sure how that can be." The words were neutral. The voice was cold. This was not Sejanus speaking to his lifelong friend; this was a Roman patrician reproving a plebe for speaking out of turn. "Perhaps you can explain it to me."

Gaius deliberately ignored that. "Marcus Volcinius is in Zhelnogra. He is overseeing a program to turn the children of Tenara away from their traditional ways and toward our Roman ways—pre-republican ways, in fact."

"I see," Sejanus said. The captain stood, and crossed the ready room to stand in front of the great window. "Go on."

"Marcus implied that these . . . these new Romans he's creating might play some important political role in the future, involving more than just Tenara. He even went so far as to claim that he was following your orders."

"Indeed."

"Does that mean that he *is* following your orders?"

"Are you questioning me? Are you requiring me to explain my motives to you?" More than ever, Sejanus was the patrician reproving the plebeian.

"By our friendship and our history, yes."

Sejanus stared at Gaius for a long moment. "Very well, then. Marcus is acting in my interest—mine, and that of Magna Roma."

"I fail to see how that can be, Captain," Gaius interrupted. "What Marcus is doing is against the laws of the Federation and against the laws of Tenara. It is dishonorable."

"Dishonorable?" Sejanus shook his head angrily. "No, it is not dishonorable. It is necessary."

Gaius folded his arms across his chest. "Explain."

Sejanus sat back in his chair and offered a smile. "Do you remember the war games we used to play, Gaius? When we were children? I was the emperor, and you my general?"

Gaius nodded.

"We could act with impunity then, with utter disregard for the consequences. We could make mistakes—die, even—but it was all make-believe." He looked into Gaius' eyes. "Do you remember?"

"I remember."

"Well, my friend, this is a game no longer. The M'dok, the Romulans, the Ferengi, follow no rules," Sejanus said. "They will destroy us unless we destroy them first. Using any method we can."

Gaius shook his head. "Any method? No, sir. A battle won without honor is a worthless victory. You knew this once—when we defeated the Romulans at Adhara. Then, you let the survivors escape, with dignity. You showed them true Roman honor."

"Escape to attack us again," Sejanus said. "I was a fool."

"No, sir. You were a hero. And now you have changed. You fight for personal glory, for your own selfish ends. Not for the good of the Federation."

Sejanus rose from his chair. "No! Now I act in the interests of the Volcinii *gens* and our world. Support me, Gaius Aldus! Join me! You'll be rewarded." He smiled. "I'm not asking you for anything new. Continue to serve me as you always have."

"You say we must destroy our enemies," Gaius said carefully. "How will you accomplish this? Picard has command here—and he will not go to war against the M'dok."

"True," Sejanus said, eyeing his first officer carefully.

And then he told Gaius what he planned to do with Captain Picard and the *Enterprise*.

"It is a bold plan," Gaius agreed when Sejanus was finished.

Sejanus turned toward him, smiling.

"But it is the plan of a madman with a callous disregard for life. I can serve you no longer, Captain," Gaius said fiercely. "You have no honor."

Sejanus stiffened at the rebuke. "And you are no Magna Roman. You disgrace the uniform you wear."

"Disgrace this uniform?" Gaius asked. He quickly drew his short sword, and Sejanus stepped back, hand moving toward his chest insignia and his communicator. Gaius' short sword darted out and flicked the captain's insignia to the ground.

Gaius stared at him for a moment—a clear look of contempt. Then he lowered his weapon. "On the contrary, it is you who disgrace this uniform, Captain. I go now to inform the Magna Roman government of your plot."

"I am ruined," Sejanus said, distress spreading across his features.

"No," Gaius said, his voice softening. "You are saved."

He reached out to take Sejanus' hand—

—and his captain reached inside his guard, drawing the short sword, and plunged it into Gaius Aldus' belly.

The first officer groaned once, a horrible noise like a giant animal gasping for breath. He grabbed hold of Sejanus' wrist, trying to loosen his hold on the sword.

But Sejanus stepped forward again, putting his weight underneath the sword, and lifted Gaius off the ground.

Gaius' eyes rolled upward in his head, and Sejanus lowered his body carefully to the ground.

"I will miss you, old friend," Sejanus said, kneeling down by his first officer's side. "But this is war."

He loosened Gaius' fingers from around his wrist and wrapped them one by one around the hilt of the sword. He held them there until Gaius' grip stiffened and his hand grew clammy.

Sejanus stood and wiped his hands clean on a towel. He picked up his communicator insignia and attached it to his chest, then touched it once, lightly.

"Security here, Captain."

"There has been an accident in my cabin. Send someone in to clean it up."

"Yes, sir."

Sejanus thought a moment. "And then get me Jenny de Luz on board the *Enterprise*."

"Captain Sejanus?" Jenny's surprised face filled the screen. "I was told you wanted to speak with me, sir."

"Yes, Jenny, I do." He paused, choosing his words carefully. "I regret to tell you that Magister Navis Gaius Aldus has dedicated his life to Magna Roma."

Jenny looked confused. "Sir? I don't—"

"I mean," Sejanus said gently, "that our beloved friend Gaius Aldus has taken his own life. He has given his soul to the state."

Slowly the meaning of the strange formal phrasing

sank in. Jenny's mouth opened. No sound came out. She stared at Sejanus, and tears filled her eyes.

"I understand your grief, child. Gaius was my oldest, closest friend," he said softly. "I am here if you need me."

Sejanus gestured, and the contact was broken.

And you will *need me,* he added silently. *Very soon.*

Chapter Thirteen

"How are you feeling, Number One?"

Riker cracked open his eyes and groaned. The last thing he remembered was Gretna screaming . . .

The M'dok.

He propped himself up on his elbows. He was in sick bay, lying on one of the diagnostic couches. Leaning over him on one side was Dr. Beverly Crusher, and on the other, his hand resting on Riker's shoulder, was Captain Jean-Luc Picard.

"Fine—I guess, sir," he said. "The attack—"

"Completely repelled, Number One. Zhelnogra is secure."

"And Gretna?"

"She's fine—in a lot better shape than you, I might add."

Riker groaned again, and turned to Dr. Crusher. "Give me the bad news, Doctor. How much longer have I got?"

"You'll live to a ripe old age," Dr. Crusher assured him. "You had a number of deep cuts here"—she pointed to Riker's chest—"and a couple bruised ribs, and your right forearm"—he looked down, and saw it was held in place by a stasis field—"was broken." She shrugged. "Just what you'd expect from a face-to-face collision with a M'dok warrior."

Picard smiled. "Perhaps I should have you take Mr. Worf's self-defense class."

"Perhaps you should have, sir." Riker returned the smile, and tried to sit up straighter. He was rewarded by a bolt of pain that shot through his chest like a knife. The captain noticed his first officer's discomfort and leaned forward to help, but Riker waved him off.

"I'm fine, sir." He took a deep breath. "Fill me in on what's been happening."

"A lot," Picard said. "And very little of it good."

The captain summarized the events of the last few days—saving the news of the Great *Saavta's* impending policy change for last.

"I still don't understand Gretna's change of heart, though, sir," Riker said when Picard had finished. "Have you been able to talk to her father about it?"

"Aah." Picard hesitated a moment. "That's a bit of bad news I had left out, Number One." He sighed heavily. "Chairman Melkinat was killed in the attack on the Great Hall."

Riker's face fell. "Oh, no."

"I'm afraid so. Which has left a thoroughly disagreeable woman named Anka as the most prominent Tenaran government official—and Gretna Melkinata has been supporting her stance."

With his good hand Riker stroked his beard thoughtfully. "What could have happened to change her mind?"

"This occurred before the M'dok attack?"

"A few days before, sir. She had stayed behind in one of the outposts . . ." He snapped his fingers. "When we met back in Zhelnogra, she mentioned something about Marcus Julius Volcinius—called him that teacher from the *Centurion.*"

"Teacher?" Picard frowned. "That man is no teacher."

"I know that, sir. Perhaps you should ask Captain Sejanus about what's going on."

Picard straightened abruptly and turned away from Riker. "I don't know, Number One. I am frankly convinced at this point that the man is not to be trusted."

"Captain Sejanus?" Riker was surprised, but said nothing.

"I'd be more inclined to find out more about Marcus ourselves," Picard said.

"Captain Picard." The voice was Deanna Troi's, and it came from the bridge.

The captain crossed to one of the companels in the wall. "Picard here."

"We've just had some rather disturbing news, sir. There's been an accident of some kind aboard the *Centurion.* Gaius Aldus is dead."

Picard and Riker exchanged surprised glances.

"Thank you, Counselor," Picard said. "I will be on the bridge immediately."

He turned back to Riker. "Something is rotten aboard that ship, Number One—and I intend to find out what it is."

223

"Good luck, sir."

"Thank you, Number One—and get well soon, will you?"

"I'll try, sir."

He was asleep, though, before Picard was completely out the door.

Picard strode crisply out of the turbolift and directly into the ready room, motioning Troi to follow him.

"Have a seat, Counselor." He gestured toward the chair in front of the desk. He raised his voice slightly. "Computer—put me through to Captain Sejanus on the *Centurion.*"

The desk screen cleared to give a view of the *Centurion*'s bridge, with Sejanus in the foreground. "Captain Picard," he said, "I assume you wish to discuss the further disposition of our forces on Tenara."

It was the first time the two captains had talked face-to-face since Picard had assumed command of their joint mission. Troi noticed that the two captains avoided pleasantries or small talk of any kind. She did not need her Betazoid abilities to sense that these two men actively disliked each other.

Picard said, "No, Captain. I need some information from you. I am surprised and distressed at the reported death of your first officer, Gaius Aldus. I would like some more information."

Sejanus' voice softened. "May I speak in confidence, Captain?"

Picard nodded. "I'm in my ready room. Your words will not go beyond the door."

"Good. I am reluctant to tell anyone the details of the story, since it does not reflect well on the Aldus family, but I know I can rely on your discretion. Poor Gaius learned just recently of a scandal involving his family. It seems an uncle of his was selling Federation secrets to the Romulans. Gaius' uncle—and quite possibly the rest of his family—faces certain imprisonment."

As he spoke, Sejanus' face grew ever more solemn.

"My *magister navis*, Captain, was perhaps a bit old-fashioned—a Roman of the old imperial school. He came to me in my cabin and told me what he had learned . . ." Sejanus' voice trailed off. "I knew he was upset, but I had no idea he intended to kill himself."

"I see." Picard nodded. "You have my deepest sympathy, Captain."

"Thank you, Captain Picard. If I might . . . I would ask you to keep a close eye on Ensign de Luz," Sejanus said. "She and Gaius had grown quite close."

"Understood. Picard out." He broke the connection and turned to Troi.

"He's lying," she said flatly. "There is much more to Gaius' death than he is telling you."

"I feel the same way." Picard hesitated, then said, "If you think it's wise to tell Ensign de Luz about this conversation, you may do so, but please do it in here."

For a moment Deanna looked puzzled. Then she remembered Picard's promise to Sejanus that what he said would not go beyond the ready room. "I'll summon her now, sir, if that's all right."

Picard nodded. "I'll leave. No, on second thought, I'll stay."

Jenny arrived within minutes. It was clear immediately that she had not been sleeping much. Her face was pale and drawn—paler even than her normal redhead's coloring—and with lines Deanna had not seen there before. Her eyes were red-rimmed, her uniform was rumpled and creased, and her hair, normally a smooth red cap, was dirty and uncombed. Still, there was a kind of bright energy in her face, but to Deanna's eye it was an unhealthy, driven kind of energy.

"Sit down, Ensign," Captain Picard said quickly.

Jenny sank gratefully into a chair. "Thank you, sir." Right away, she turned to Deanna Troi. "Do you have any news for me?"

"Ensign—Jenny—the captain and I tried to find out the details of Gaius Aldus' death, as I promised you." She told Jenny what Sejanus had said.

"His uncle betrayed the Federation? And so Gaius killed himself?"

"That's what Sejanus told us, Jenny," Deanna said. "Do you have any reason to doubt that?"

Jenny shook her head.

"Had Gaius given you any hints of trouble aboard the *Centurion,* or with Captain Sejanus?" Picard asked.

"No," Jenny said quietly. She stared at the floor silently for a moment. "If that's all, may I go, sir?"

"Of course." Picard smiled gently. "And take the next couple of days off, Ensign. Give yourself some rest."

* * *

"Captain Sejanus?"

"Hmmm?" The aide's voice had startled him; Sejanus had been preparing for bed, and was unaccustomed to interruption.

"Captain, someone from the *Enterprise* is here to speak with you. An ensign." The aide's voice carried an overtone of disapproval.

"Ensign de Luz?" Sejanus asked, the fatigue vanishing from his mind. Instinctively he could feel the importance of the call.

"Yes, Captain," the aide replied, sounding somewhat surprised.

"Where is she now?"

"In the transporter room, Captain."

"Have her brought here, Lieutenant. Immediately."

Sejanus had just finished dressing when the chime rang. "Come," he said, sitting on his bed.

The door slid open and Jenny walked in. Sejanus was immediately struck by the difference in her appearance. She was clearly exhausted, her face lined with worry and pain. But somehow she glowed with energy, her eyes oddly luminous.

He had never thought of her as attractive before, but now . . .

"Ensign de Luz reporting, sir." Her voice was very distant.

"At ease, Ensign. Jenny. Please, relax."

She moved from attention to a stance with her feet shoulder-width apart, her hands clasped at the small of her back, her upper body still ramrod-straight, and her eyes staring straight ahead—the textbook definition of "at ease," and not what Sejanus had had in mind. "How can I help you, Jenny?"

"Gaius Aldus . . ."

Jenny had closed her eyes, and she was shaking; after a moment, Sejanus realized that she was crying. He rose from the bed and took her into his arms, holding her tightly as she wept.

After a little while he pushed her away slightly, still holding her shoulders, and looked into her eyes. "Listen to me, Jenny," he said gently. "Gaius' death was a tragedy, and I feel his loss no less keenly than you. But we must put him behind us and look to other things, to the future."

"I know that," she said, avoiding his eyes.

"Look." He led her to a chair, helped her sit down, and stood beside her. In front of them, on his desk, was an empty computer screen. "Computer," he said. "Roma, the Regia."

Onto the computer screen there came the image of a great city, the view focusing upon a large building fronted by massive pillars, magnificently decorated. Men in togas were walking in and out of the building, looking like insects in comparison to the gargantuan structure.

"This is the Regia Republicae, the Palace of the Republic, our capitol. It occupies the entire top of the hill we call the Palatium. It's where the Senate meets and the center of government on Magna Roma. This is where the power lies!" He turned her chair around, gazing down at her.

"That hill, that complex of buildings"—he gestured toward the screen—"used to be called simply the Regia, the Palace, and everyone understood that that meant the Palace of the Emperor. My namesake's palace, Jenny! Augustus built his palace up there, and then Tiberius built one near it, but it was the Emperor Sejanus who completed the complex and made the Palatium the true center of the empire. For two thousand years it was the seat of the emperors, the center of the empire, and then the center of the world. For two thousand years, until the republic, and even now it is still the true center of power. It is the crowning achievement of our civilization, yet it is in danger of falling—in the same way Tenara has."

He clasped his hands behind his back and began pacing. "Jenny, the M'dok grow bolder with each attack. The next time they strike, we must deliver them a crushing blow—a blow that will send them scurrying back to the safety of their own borders. The *Centurion* alone is not powerful enough to deliver that blow. I need the *Enterprise*'s firepower on my side to do that."

Jenny swallowed. "I'm with you, sir . . . but there is little I can do to help you."

"On the contrary, Jenny." He faced her. "You hold the key to our chances against the M'dok." He crossed to the computer on his desk and brought up a display of the *Centurion*'s defensive systems.

"Look how intricate my ship's defenses are. No one man can possibly coordinate them. It takes the thinking power of a computer—and in any battle involving more than one ship, the problems of maintaining a coherent offensive and defensive strategy multiply exponentially. One ship's computer must take command of all the others—a procedure accomplished through the use of a simple six-digit number called a prefix code.

"We talked before about the Romans who sacrificed themselves for the safety of the empire—who were unafraid to stand up for what they thought was right. Now I want you to stand up for what you believe in, Jenny." He gazed into her eyes. "I want you to obtain the *Enterprise*'s prefix code for me. So that the next time the M'dok attack Tenara, I have control of the *Enterprise.*"

For a long moment Jenny was silent, staring at the computer screen, deliberately avoiding Sejanus' gaze.

Then she straightened, and nodded. "You'll have that code, sir. On my honor, I swear it."

Sejanus nodded, and allowed himself a small smile. He had won.

He would use the code to lower the *Enterprise*'s shields, and destroy her himself. His engineers on board the ship were even now sabotaging the larger vessel's phaser banks, destroying her ability to fight back. The M'dok, of course, would be blamed—and that would bring on the war he needed to catapult him to glory, to the command of his planet . . .

. . . and perhaps beyond.

"Is there anything else I can do, sir?" Jenny asked.

He was about to dismiss her, then noticed Jenny's eyes gleaming darkly, luminously at him. By God, she was beautiful! If nothing else, Gaius had shown excellent taste.

Perhaps there *was* something else she could do for him.

"Jenny," he said urgently, "there's a great adventure ahead of me. Join me. I know you: nothing is beyond you. Be my *magistra navis,* stand beside me, command my forces."

He bent toward her, touching his lips gently to hers.

With a passion that surprised him, Jenny returned his kiss.

"Gaius Aldus! Commit suicide!" Worf shook his head. "Never, sir."

It was the following morning, and Picard was on the bridge, having just brought his security chief, down on the planet's surface, up-to-date on recent events.

"Go on, Lieutenant."

Worf's image, on the main viewscreen, said, "I was with him yesterday, and he seemed in fine spirits." The Klingon paused. "That is, until Marcus Julius showed up."

Picard's eyebrows rose. "Marcus Julius Volcinius? That man's name seems to be cropping up everywhere, Lieutenant." He thought a moment. "See if you can locate Marcus yourself, Lieutenant Worf. And find out what he knows about Gaius' death."

Worf grinned, revealing two rows of sharp, even teeth.

"It will be my pleasure, sir."

Marcus Volcinius, in his brand-new sumptuous house in Zhelnogra, was feeling rather pleased with himself. He was ahead of the schedule he had proposed to his cousin. Tomorrow he would begin the organization of what he intended to call the Young Romans League.

He was wearing the ornately embroidered toga he would wear the next day when he addressed the new organization. On his desk before him was a sheet of paper on which he was drawing various possible standards that the Young Romans would carry during their frequent parades. At this point, the words of the League's charter were still vague, but he knew they'd come to him. This kind of organizing was certainly his talent, what the gods had made him for. In the future—the future planned by Sejanus—there would be even more avenues for that talent.

The sound of a knock on the door interrupted his pleasant reverie.

"Come in," he said. He was expecting Julius Apius, his personal assistant.

"Now, Julius," he said, not bothering to look up, "I need you to arrange for another case of the local ale—the *jhafre*—to be brought here immediately. The first one is simply unsatisfactory, and—"

"Excuse me."

That was not Julius' voice.

He looked up—and saw Lieutenant Worf from the *Enterprise* standing in front of his desk, hands folded behind his back.

"I was told I might find you here," Worf said. "If you have a moment, I would like to discuss several matters with you."

Marcus glanced quickly at the old-fashioned clock hanging on the wall behind Worf.

"I find I am running late for an appointment,

Lieutenant." He rose and pushed his chair back from the desk. "Perhaps tomorrow afternoon . . ."

Worf turned and noticed the clock. "Hmmm," he said, taking it down off the wall and examining it closely. "Your clock is running fast." He turned the hands back a full hour. "Now it shows the correct time."

The Klingon pulled up a chair and sat down in front of Marcus' desk. "Now, I would like you to tell me about Gaius Aldus—what happened to him after you two left me."

"Ensign de Luz calling, sir."

Sejanus rose from his desk. "Put this on a closed channel, Ensign. In my quarters only."

"Aye, sir."

Sejanus strode quickly to the small monitor in his quarters and activated it.

"I have the information you requested, Captain," Jenny said. Her eyes shone with excitement.

"Excellent. Beam over at once."

Jenny shook her head. "It would seem too suspicious. I will rendezvous with you on the planet's surface in one hour." She gave him a set of coordinates outside the city.

Sejanus nodded to himself. The fewer people who knew he had been meeting with an *Enterprise* crew member before that ship's untimely destruction, the better. "Very well. Sejanus out."

He placed another call to his personal guard, to alert the engineers aboard the *Enterprise* to stand ready.

Chapter Fourteen

"THAT IS a very interesting story," Worf said calmly. "Now I would like to hear the truth."

"What I've told you is the truth, Lieutenant," Marcus insisted. He raised his right hand and held it out so that his palm was facing Worf. "I swear it—upon my honor as a Roman."

Worf frowned in disapproval. "Then we Klingons have a much different code of honor than Magna Romans. We would never swear to such a transparent lie."

Marcus wiped his brow. The Klingon had remained virtually motionless in his chair for the last five minutes while Marcus spun a tale of how Gaius Aldus and he had gone to a brief meeting with a group of Tenaran farmers. Now Worf glanced briefly at the clock behind him again, and spoke in a disapproving tone.

"I see your clock is beginning to run fast once more."

But while the Klingon's attention was elsewhere, Marcus had extended one hand below his desk, eased open a drawer, and reached inside.

"I don't know what you want from me, Lieutenant," the Magna Roman said, "but I assure you—"

He drew the phaser that had been hidden in his desk and held it in front of him with both hands, pointing it directly at Worf.

"—that you are not going to get it."

He would have to kill the Klingon, of course—but how to explain his disappearance? Then he remembered; it would not matter. His captain's plan called for the disappearance of the entire *Enterprise* crew.

He laughed.

Worf shook his head reproachfully. "I know you are not threatening me with that phaser," he said. "That would be a foolish thing to do."

"Oh?" Marcus raised an eyebrow. "How so?"

"It is very simple," Worf continued. "That is a type-I phaser—currently turned to setting three. Powerful enough to stun most humanoids, but unfortunately for you"—and here he smiled—"we Klingons are not most humanoids."

Marcus' own grin wavered slightly.

"Of course," Worf continued, "you could change the current setting. But that would take you at least two seconds, during which time I would surely—"

Marcus glanced for a split second at the phaser, sliding his thumb forward . . .

. . . and Worf bounded over the desk in one easy motion, ripping the phaser out of Marcus' grasp as easily as if he was disarming a child.

"—overpower you," Worf finished, sitting back in his chair again. "I was wrong. It took you only one second to change the setting on the phaser." He smiled. "Congratulations."

Marcus nodded dumbly.

"Now, tell me about Gaius Aldus," he said. "The truth. Or perhaps you would like to experience some of the physical discomfort I promised you earlier . . ."

Marcus slumped disconsolately over his desk and began to talk.

The Tenaran plains were dusty and dry, and the wind was high.

Jenny blinked back tears from irritated eyes as she waited for Sejanus.

He materialized about a meter in front of her, dressed in Roman armor instead of a Starfleet uniform.

"Jenny," he said, stepping toward her. He took her hands in his, and smiled. "Do you have the prefix code for me?"

"Yes, I do. But first I want to know something."

"Of course." Sejanus nodded. "What is it?"

Jenny let her hands drop to her sides and stared the *Centurion*'s captain in the face. "Why did Gaius kill himself?"

"Why did . . .? Well . . ." He cleared his throat. "I assumed Captain Picard had told you. A family scandal." He looked directly at her. "To talk of it now . . . brings me pain. You do understand, don't you?"

"Of course," Jenny said quietly. "It brings me pain too."

Her gaze left Sejanus' face and seemed to focus beyond the horizon, into empty space. When she spoke again, her voice was harsh and empty of feeling. "Because when Gaius and I first met, you see, he told me he had no family. No one in the world at all—but you."

She turned back to Sejanus, and now she couldn't keep the tears from her eyes. "He loved you. And you killed him—just as surely as if you had driven the sword through him with your own hand."

"That's nonsense," Sejanus said coldly. "Utter nonsense."

"Then why the lie about his family? Why *did* he kill himself?"

In response, Sejanus moved closer to her and placed his hands on her shoulders. "Forget him, Jenny. You and I are what is important now. The things we can achieve together . . ."

She closed her eyes, shaking her head, pulling away from him. "You still don't understand, Captain Sejanus." Her eyes snapped open. "Captain, in my capacity as an officer of Starfleet security, I am placing you under arrest, relieving you of duty until such time as you may be brought to trial. You are charged with conspiring to overthrow by force the democratically elected government of a Federation member world."

"Jenny . . ." He stepped forward, offering her his hand. "Come with me. Stand by my side. You can have power, glory, everything—"

She cut him off. "I don't want your power," she said, spitting out each word, "and I don't want you."

"Then you're a fool," he said, reaching for his sword. "And you will have to die a fool's death—just as Gaius Aldus did."

Jenny stared at him unbelievingly for a second.

And then she went mad.

There was very little of Starfleet training in her attack, and nothing of discipline. She was the daughter of an ancient warrior family of Meramar, of a people accustomed to fighting their way to what they wanted through blood and war, and it was this tradition that sent the adrenaline pouring through her in a burst of freezing flame, sent her hands reaching for Sejanus' throat.

He stepped back, hand around the gladius hanging by his side; before he could do more than draw it halfway, her foot smashed into his wrist, and then she was on him.

He was knocked to the ground by her furious attack, landing with her hands already locked around his neck. He grabbed her wrists, trying to force her hands back, trying to breathe.

Slowly the pressure lessened, and he gained enough leverage to pull his leg out from under her, placing his knee against her belly and pushing. Even as she was lifted off him, she struck down like a snake, fastening her teeth in his arm, and then they were rolling over and over in the dirt, each trying desperately to gain an advantage over the other.

His superior size and weight told heavily in this type of fighting. In the end, though cut and bruised, he was on top of her, holding her wrists with one hand, while the other drew back for a brutal punch to the side of her face.

The Roman struck her with a fury as great as hers, uncontrolled animal brutality, for that was his way. Both of them children of warrior worlds, they had both lost control in the rush of blood lust.

And suddenly Jenny was clearly, coldly sane.

It's the warrior's way. It's Sejanus' way. But not Starfleet's way, not Captain Picard's—and not mine! She could win, she knew, if she fought as she had been trained. Even as he was preparing to hit her again, she shifted under him, finding the weak point in his balance and throwing him off in a single convulsive movement.

Before he could rise, she lashed out with a snap kick, catching him in the face, and then leapt to her feet. He rose almost as quickly, stretching out his hands and roaring as he charged for her.

It could hardly have been simpler. She stepped aside, dodging him easily, and delivered a vicious kidney punch before catching him in the stomach with a powerful roundhouse kick.

Holding his side, he wheeled and charged her again. This time she did not step aside; instead, she met him squarely, stepping forward and driving a side kick straight into his chin.

The shock jarred her, but Sejanus fell to the ground, trying weakly to rise and then collapsing, semiconscious.

She stood there sucking in great gasps of the clean, cold air, standing over her fallen opponent.

Then she reached up to her communicator.

"De Luz to *Enterprise*," she told them. "Two to beam up." And then she threw back her head and looked to the sky as her body dissolved in the transporter beam.

"Lieutenant Worf calling from the planet's surface, sir."

"Put him on-screen," Picard snapped. He'd just had another frustrating day of discussions with the Great *Saavta*—and another angry exchange with its hard-line members over the need for Federation defenses on Tenara.

The captain leaned forward in his chair, hoping for good news.

Worf's face appeared on the main viewscreen at the front of the bridge.

"Any progress, Lieutenant?"

"Yes, sir," Worf replied. "I found Marcus Volcinius, sir—and some very interesting information."

Captain Picard listened intently as Worf relayed the information Marcus had given him.

"Well done," Picard said when he was finished. "Bring your prisoner aboard ship, and then I think we'll arrange another meeting with the Tenarans."

"Yes, sir." The Klingon's image faded from the viewscreen.

Picard smacked his hands together in satisfaction, and sat down again.

"Get Sejanus on the *Centurion* for me, and—"

"No need, Captain."

Picard spun.

Jenny de Luz stood in the turbolift, her hair disheveled, her uniform torn and dirty, her face bruised.

"Captain Sejanus is in the brig." She smiled. "And I am reporting in—fit for duty, sir."

Picard walked slowly up to the deck in front of the turbolift and studied Jenny for a moment before he spoke.

"Yes, you are, Ensign." He smiled. "And we're glad to have you back."

When he had to, Geordi La Forge could move.

And judging from what little Captain Picard had told him, he had to move now. When he reached the turbolift, his heart was pounding madly; he had covered the short distance from his quarters with a speed that would have surprised some of the best runners in the Federation. The human ones, anyway.

Data, whom Picard had also alerted, was already in the turbolift, waiting.

"Engineering," Geordi gasped as he leaned against the turbolift door. He shook his head. "Appius Cornelius and his Magna Romans have been crawling all over this ship for days. They've probably got the engines halfway dismantled by now!"

"I hardly think that likely, Geordi," Data began. "Were that the case, we surely would have noticed—"

Geordi shook his head, just as the turbolift doors slid open.

Simultaneously, the turbolift doors on the other side of engineering opened, and three security officers stepped out, their phasers drawn.

The *Centurion* personnel who had been working on

the *Enterprise* systems looked up, startled. As the security guards approached them, most simply raised their hands over their heads, but one grabbed a heavy tool and swung at the head of one of the security officers.

There was no time to react, and Geordi gasped, expecting to see the officer's head laid open—and then an arm suddenly appeared between the tool and the officer's head, stopping the blow with ease.

Data smiled pleasantly, showing no sign of pain from a blow that would have broken a human's arm. He removed the tool from the Roman's grasp and crumpled it with one hand.

"I believe the appropriate phrase is 'Surrender or die,'" Data said.

Geordi laughed. "You've been reading too many old detective stories, Data. No one says that anymore!"

"Why not?" Data asked, turning back toward the Roman, who had his hands held high and clearly intended to offer no further resistance.

"It seems to work quite well."

Worf stood behind Picard on the bridge now, watching the image of the *Centurion* floating in space.

"Captain, we have a message from the *Centurion*."

"On-screen, Lieutenant."

The ship disappeared, and its place was taken by a burly, aggressive-looking man wearing a cloak over a gold-colored uniform, with commander's rank on his collar.

"Captain Picard, I am Commander Claudius Marcellus Caecus, *Centurion* chief of security and acting captain. I demand to know what has happened to Captain Sejanus."

How typical of Sejanus, Picard thought sadly, that his security chief should be so high in the chain of command.

"Commander Caecus, I regret to inform you that your captain has been placed into custody."

Caecus' eyes went wide. "On what charges? And by whose authority?"

"He has broken countless Starfleet regulations, not the least of which is the Prime Directive," Picard said flatly. "We will keep him on board the *Enterprise* until such time as we can release him into Starfleet custody at Starbase 16. Furthermore, if I have anything to say about it, Commander, and I shall"—he rose from his command chair, his powerful voice ringing out across the bridge—"he will be court-martialed!"

Caecus' image abruptly disappeared, to be replaced by a starfield, with the *Centurion* floating before them. As they watched, the smaller ship's impulse engines glowed, and she accelerated away from them.

"Should I follow them, sir?" Wesley asked from the helm.

Picard shook his head. "No, Mr. Crusher, not now. But track them."

Wesley tapped some controls, then shrugged. "They've disappeared around Tenara, sir. And the satellites aren't tracking them."

"Very clever," Picard said, steepling his fingers. "The *Centurion* doesn't register on the satellites' sensors, so we have no idea where they are or what they're doing. How did they manage that, I wonder."

Almost simultaneously, Data and Wesley turned around and said, "The subspace transtator wavelengths can be—"

Picard held up his hand. "A technical explanation can wait, gentlemen. What's really important is how long they've been doing that, and what they've been doing in the meantime. Worf, have Captain Sejanus brought to the bridge."

Several things then happened simultaneously.

The *Centurion* appeared suddenly from behind the Tenaran moon, her phasers glowing with contained energy. Without pause or warning, she opened fire.

The *Enterprise* was totally unprepared, but Starfleet designers had made the starship well. The low-level navigational shields, which protected the great ship from space debris, absorbed some of the energy. The immensely fast ship's computer should have done the rest. It calculated in a picosecond the direction of fire, how much power would be needed to counteract it, and how much would inevitably get through. Normally that would have been sufficient safeguard to prevent damage. However, Appius Cornelius' men had done their work well, and there had simply not been time enough for the engineers under Geordi La Forge's command to find all of the Magna Romans' sabotage. Despite the automatic signal from the *Enterprise* computer, very little extra energy was fed to the shields at the impact point.

The *Centurion*'s shot had been aimed at the juncture between the main saucer section and the warp drive section, resulting in a minimum of casualties, but totally disrupting power throughout the entire ship for a little over five seconds.

Which was all the time Sejanus, down in the brig, needed.

The *Centurion*'s captain had always been quick to take advantage of fortunate accidents. As quick as thought, his powerful legs pushed hard against the wall and sent him flying out into the corridor.

The lights and security force field came on just as Sejanus cleared the doorway to his cell. He felt a tingling in his feet and looked down to see that the soles of his boots were smoking. It had been a near thing.

He rolled to his feet. No guards had been posted. Foolish.

He ran down the corridor, and as he ran, he slapped the control plates on the outside of the other cells holding prisoners from the *Centurion,* releasing them. There was a good-sized pack following him by the time he was done.

Sejanus gathered them together. "Is this everyone?" he asked.

One of the Magna Roman engineers spoke up. "All of us except for Appius Cornelius, sir. They took him to sick bay."

"Most unfortunate," Sejanus said brusquely. Appius was—had been—one of his better operatives. A pity that he had to be left behind, but Sejanus had never wasted time on vain regret. "Follow me," he ordered.

Together they sprinted for the transporter room.

"Sir!" Data said sharply. "My displays show transporters being activated!"

"Cut power to the transporter room, Mr. Data!" Picard ordered immediately.

Data's fingers flew over his console—but even as he worked, the android was shaking his head.

"It is too late, sir. A full load was beamed over to the *Centurion.*"

"Sejanus," Picard said. He cursed himself for not posting guards outside the brig.

"I am detecting an energy buildup from the *Centurion,* sir," Data added.

"*Centurion* firing photon torpedoes, sir!" Worf said.

"Evasive action!" Picard cried, bracing himself. The whole structure of the ship shook slightly as the powerful engines kicked in full force.

But the torpedoes had not been intended to damage the *Enterprise.* They detonated several hundred kilometers in front of the great ship, momentarily filling the main viewer with a brilliant burst of blue-white light.

When the explosion faded, the *Centurion* was gone.

"Can you follow them, Mr. Crusher?"

Wesley shook his head. "They left at maximum warp, sir. There's no way to tell where they are now."

Picard nodded; he had expected no other answer.

"Lieutenant Worf, prepare messages for Starfleet

Command and the Senate of Magna Roma, informing them of the *Centurion*'s disappearance and Captain Sejanus' plans." He stood. "Mr. Data, you have the conn."

Picard headed for the turbolift and his cabin—and some much-needed rest.

Epilogue

SEVERAL HOURS LATER, Worf went off duty, having finished transmitting the last of Captain Picard's messages to Starfleet Command. Coded, of course—regulation procedure in a situation where hostiles could be monitoring communications.

When he returned to his quarters, he found a message waiting for him from Jenny de Luz.

He first thought of calling in Deanna Troi. But Jenny was his subordinate, his responsibility. He had recommended her for the duty on Tenara that had led to her involvement with Gaius Aldus in the first place. "Computer," he said, "get me Ensign Jenny de Luz."

"Ensign de Luz is on Holodeck Three," the computer answered. "You are now in contact."

"Jenny, this is Lieutenant Worf."

"I have something to ask you, Lieutenant." Her voice was strong and purposeful, not at all what he expected. "Could you meet me here on the holodeck?"

Worf nodded. "I'm on my way."

When he reached Holodeck Three, there was no sign of Jenny, and he realized she must be waiting inside for him. He entered to find himself in the middle of a simulation.

Before him was a flat plain stretching to a distant horizon. The tip of the rising sun showed over the horizon, growing slowly in the overcast sky. To his left was a heavy forest, and to his right was a hill, its top crowned by a massive building. Ringing the hill was a camp, with men strolling about or standing in clumps talking. Every now and then, some of them would look up at the building on the hilltop and then resume their conversations. Jenny stood a short distance in front of him, watching his reactions.

"Welcome to Meramar, Lieutenant," she said. "I've spent the last couple of hours getting the details right. What do you think of it?"

"A harsh environment," Worf said.

"Very harsh. That's where I grew up." Jenny pointed at the hilltop. "Castle de Luz, which makes it sound a lot grander than it really was. And that"—she pointed at the encampment—"is the army of my father's cousin, Domin Hame de Luz, which is laying siege to the castle."

"Siege!" Worf exclaimed. "In this day and age? With modern weapons, that's a meaningless word."

Jenny shook her head. "Not if all the parties agree to limit themselves to the weapons of the first settlers brought here by the Preservers. This siege happened when I was three years old. It was finally settled by single combat between my father and his cousin. My father won. I can still remember his wounds. And the head of his cousin decorating the great dining hall for a few days. Fortunately it was winter."

"Barbaric."

Jenny grinned suddenly. "Remind you of another world?"

Worf said stiffly, "Klingons were not barbarians. They reacted to a grim environment with a grim social code in order to survive. And then in the end they outgrew even that code and joined the Federation."

"Yes. Exactly the same thing happened on Meramar. My ancestors evolved a grim code too, to survive. They joined the Federation, but the social code has scarcely changed."

Worf felt off-balance. "Ensign, you're not there anymore. This is a simulation. Problems aren't settled here on the *Enterprise* by means of single combat."

Jenny nodded soberly. "I know that, sir. But I'm a product of this world. It's part of me. I came here to try to understand something about myself. The battle between my father and his cousin is about to begin. Right now, my father is up there in his castle, in the chapel, dedicating his weapons and his soul to Servado and praying for victory. It's an ancient ceremony. And this time I'll be able to watch the whole thing with a lot more understanding than when I was three years old."

A shout arose from the camp at the base of the hill, and suddenly the camp came alive, men running toward a central point. Jenny smiled, her face transformed by eagerness. "Do you hear that, Lieutenant? It's about to begin. My father is about to come down the hillside and settle the old feud."

"You said you had something to ask me, Ensign. I have no interest in watching two men try to kill each other." He turned to go.

"Computer," Jenny called out, "freeze simulation."

The shouts from the camp stopped abruptly. Worf turned back to Jenny. "Well?"

"First I have to correct you, Lieutenant," Jenny said, as if she were discussing a completely neutral topic. "It's not two men trying to kill each other: it's two men trying, and one succeeding." She took a deep breath. "I want you to put me on special assignment. I want to find Captain Sejanus."

Worf shook his head slowly. Despite the abrupt change of subject, he was not surprised. "So you can kill him?"

"So I can bring him back to stand trial for the murder of Gaius Aldus!" Jenny shouted.

Worf shook his head. "How will you bring Sejanus to justice? He has disappeared—and it is a very large galaxy, Ensign."

"I'll find him," Jenny said simply. "I'll find him."

"Indeed," Worf said. "Then I wish you luck. But why did you call me here?"

"I thought you might want to help."

"I do," Worf said. "But my duty is here aboard this starship, Ensign. Not chasing vengeance across the galaxy."

"I . . ." Jenny said, and then she broke, began sobbing.

There was nothing in the manual about how to cover this situation, so Worf acted instinctively. He growled, and reluctantly allowed Jenny to lean on him as she cried.

"I'm glad you could come," Will Riker said. He reached out with his good arm, taking Gretna's hand and helping her down off the transporter platform.

"Will," she said, looking at him in shock. "Your arm—"

"Is fine," he assured her. "It'll be good as new in another day or two. Now, come on—and I'll show you how Marcus tricked you."

He led her down the corridor and into the turbolift.

"Deck Four," he said. The car began moving.

"So," he began, turning to Gretna and smiling, "how do you like the *Enterprise?*"

"It seems wonderful. I'm very excited to be here, especially if what you told me about this . . ." She faltered, looking for the word.

"Holodeck," Riker supplied.

". . . holodeck is true."

"It may sound like a miracle, but I assure you, it's quite real."

"I'm afraid I still don't understand how they got the doubles to sound and behave just like real people."

"They're not doubles. The holodeck is run by a sophisticated computer program, which they—Marcus and Sejanus—simply told what to do."

The turbolift doors opened, and Riker led Gretna down the corridor to the holodeck entrance.

"Now," Riker said, "what you'll first see is a completely empty room—but whatever you want to make real in there, you can. Anything is possible in this room. Anything."

Riker touched the control panel, and the door slid open—revealing Lieutenant Worf holding Jenny de Luz in his arms.

Riker smothered a laugh.

"Excuse me, Ensign, Commander," Worf said, detaching himself from Jenny. He strode determinedly past them into the corridor beyond.

Jenny was just a few seconds behind him, looking just as uncomfortable. "Commander, ma'am."

And she was gone as well, the holodeck door sliding shut behind her.

"I think we interrupted something," Riker said.

"I think so too. Will, what is this place?"

"I don't know, but it's beautiful."

"It's like we're on another world," Gretna said, turning to take in the entire holodeck illusion. "And you could make images of people as well?"

Riker nodded.

"My father and Captain Picard?"

"I could," Riker said gently. "Would you like me to?"

"No," she said quickly, then lowered her gaze. "Will, I feel like such a fool. I should have talked to you before about what Marcus said, not been so quick to believe him."

He shook his head. "It doesn't matter now."

"But it does," Gretna said. "Can you forgive me?"

Riker smiled. "Well . . . anything is possible," he said, taking her in his arms. "Especially in here."

* * *

There was still too much to understand.

Jean-Luc Picard, scholar, scientist, diplomat, and sometime soldier, drummed his fingers on the tabletop in his quarters as he tried to comprehend it all.

The M'dok had at last responded to Federation overtures—Picard felt confident their murderous raids would soon end. The Magna Roman government was itself in the midst of a massive shake-up, sparked by these latest revelations about the Volcinii *gens*. And Sejanus . . .

He was out there somewhere, Picard knew, still pursuing his ambitions, undoubtedly planning to pursue his mad dreams, to reclaim his lost honor.

Picard doubted that he would ever know exactly what motivations had driven Captain Lucius Aelius Sejanus. That Sejanus was truly a madman, Picard did not doubt—but underlying the madness there had been a brilliance and a capacity to make things happen of a sort which altered the course of civilizations.

Alexander, Picard thought. Julius Caesar. Saladin. Napoleon. Gandhi. Hitler. Schroeder. Colonel Green. Kahless. Cochrane. Surak. Tagore.

It's such a fine line . . .

Perhaps, as well, it was another case of power corrupting? For Magna Roma to leap from the equivalent of twentieth to twenty-fourth century Earth technology in eighty years had to be a heady, destabilizing experience. To find oneself with so much power, so quickly . . .

It could change a man—even one who had passed Starfleet's strict psychological tests.

And yet there was more.

For within Captain Sejanus there had also been something else which, perhaps, only Captain Picard could fully understand.

It was nothing he could name, nor did he want to.

"But in Lucius Aelius Sejanus," he whispered aloud into the silence of his cabin, "there was much of Jean-Luc Picard."

He stared at his desk, at his hands lying folded atop it.

Our hands and our minds, he thought. These are what make us human. What our minds can imagine, for good or ill, our hands can build. And from then on, there are no limits.

Outside the *Enterprise* were uncounted gleaming stars, and things that had yet to be understood, and the absolute silence of space.